STRANGLEHOLD

STRANGLEHOLD

WITHDRAWN

ED GORMAN

THORNDIKE
CHIVERS

This Large Print edition is published by Thorndike Press, Waterville, Maine, USA and by AudioGO Ltd, Bath, England.
Thorndike Press, a part of Gale, Cengage Learning.

The text of this Large Print edition is unabridged.
Other aspects of the book may vary from the original edition.
Set in 16 pt. Plantin.

LIBRARY OF CONGRESS CATALOGING-IN-PUBLICATION DATA

Gorman, Ed.
    Stranglehold / by Ed Gorman.
        p. cm. — (Thorndike Press large print mystery)
    ISBN-13: 978-1-4104-3361-9
    ISBN-10: 1-4104-3361-7
    1. Legislators—United States—Fiction. 2. Political campaigns—Fiction. 3. United States—Politics and government—Fiction. 4. Large type books. I. Title.
PS3557.O759S77 2011
813'.54—dc22   2010044441

BRITISH LIBRARY CATALOGUING-IN-PUBLICATION DATA AVAILABLE
Published in 2011 in the U.S. by arrangement with St. Martin's Press, LLC.
Published in 2011 in the U.K. by arrangement with the author.

U.K. Hardcover: 978 1 445 83626 3 (Chivers Large Print)
U.K. Softcover: 978 1 445 83627 0 (Camden Large Print)

Printed in the United States of America
1 2 3 4 5 6 7 15 14 13 12 11

To my son Joe,
a wiser man
than I'll ever be,
with love and admiration

ACKNOWLEDGMENTS

I want to thank my friend and colleague Linda Siebels for her usual hard work on this manuscript.

I also want to thank the International Myeloma Foundation for the information and research that gives hope to all of us with the incurable cancer multiple myeloma.

Whenever a man has cast a longing eye on offices, a rottenness begins in his conduct.

— Thomas Jefferson

Under democracy, one party always devotes its chief energies to trying to prove that the other party is unfit to rule — and both commonly succeed, and are right.

— H. L. Mencken

PART ONE

CHAPTER 1

All roads lead to motels. A private detective told me that once, and I remembered it as I watched Susan Cooper, United States Congresswoman Susan Cooper, aim her green Volvo into the last parking slot on the west side of the Family Inn.

The date was the second of October, which meant we were about one month away from the election. As a political consultant, I divide my life up by election cycles. And I was worried that this cycle might see the end of Susan's political career, for which my Chicago office was largely responsible.

I wore a Cubs cap and sunglasses and drove a rental car — a scruffy disguise. I'd followed her through Aldyne, the Illinois city where her family name was still formidable. Though I wasn't handling her campaign personally — I was working on a gubernatorial campaign in Michigan — a call to me yesterday afternoon had made her reelection campaign my problem.

The motel was on the south end of the city. The noontime sunlight was welcome but not warm.

After getting out of the Volvo, Susan stood on the walk looking around, a graceful blond woman in a well-tailored navy-blue suit and conservative black heels. She had the kind of face that had been chic for thousands of years. The family fortune had allowed her to go to Smith and learn how to dress handsomely without making too fine a point of it.

She continued to look around. If she'd been in an acting class, I would have guessed that her instructor had just told her to look frightened because she sure as hell did. A man and woman emerged from a room three doors down from where she stood. She turned away from them so they wouldn't be able to see her face. After all, this was her hometown and she was its congresswoman.

The couple headed for a once-red Dodge with a cracked windshield and a broken taillight. They carried their belongings in duffel bags. They paid no attention to her.

After their Dodge disappeared, Susan spent another minute glancing around again before making her move to the door at the end of the walk. She moved quickly now. Furtively.

I watched all this from the parking lot of a McDonald's that flowed into the motel lot. It was lunchtime, and with all the traffic in and out she didn't notice me.

Apparently, the investors behind the motel had decided to spend most of their money on other projects. The macadam was cracked in places; a few of the windows had tape covering cracks; and the red-brick facing was filthy. I doubted this was the kind of place Susan Cooper frequented very often.

She knocked on the door. As she waited for a response, she started looking around again. I thought she had spotted me as she surveyed the merged parking lots, but her eyes moved on past me.

Ben Weinberg was running this campaign for my firm. He'd told me that for the past few weeks Congresswoman Cooper had been disappearing twice a week and had acted nervous, even distraught, when she returned. This was damaging her campaign. She'd been in a debate three weeks ago that had made her look unprepared and irritable. Internal and external polling showed that even her admirers thought she'd done poorly and wondered if something was wrong with her.

Our opponent, a man named Steve Duffy, was outspending us two-to-one and was starting to close in on us. Susan Cooper was a distraction for me, but Weinberg had insisted that I spend a few days here trying to find out what was bothering the congresswoman even though she refused to acknowledge that anything *was* bothering her. Weinberg had tried following her once himself. He hadn't been good at it. She'd figured it out after only twenty minutes or so, pulled over to the shoulder of the road, and waved him to stop. According to him, Susan had come close to firing him.

She knocked again, but this time the door swung inward. Apparently, it hadn't been closed or locked. She went inside.

For the next ten minutes I listened to NPR. The reporter was discussing all the jobs that had been lost in the past two weeks. He raised the most frequently asked question among talking heads: Are we already in a real depression? Just today three major corporations had laid off a total of twenty-four thousand people. With statistics like that, this should be an easy win for us, but Duffy was smart, good-natured, and appealing. He believed in the holy creed his side had been pushing for more than a century, but he dispensed it with smiles. There wouldn't be any landslides here. Victory would be close.

She came out quickly. She tried to close the door, but it appeared to be resisting. She gave it a sharp tug, but I could see that it still wasn't closed right.

This time she didn't look around. She walked right to her Volvo, opened the door, slid inside. She put her head to the curve of the steering wheel and stayed that way for a brief time.

The brake lights flared and she started to back out. A van from a local electric company was behind her as she hit the gas. He leaned on the horn. She slammed on her brakes. She fluttered him a wave of apology. Her head dropped down. I wondered if she was crying. Or if she was going to lay her head against the steering wheel again.

When the van passed, she backed out, this time slowly. I could almost feel her forcing herself to get control of the moment. She pointed her car to the exit and left.

There wasn't any point in following her. Something had happened in the motel room, and I needed to know what it had been.

My instinct after so many years in army intelligence was to reach for the glove compartment, where I'd stashed my Glock. I had a license to carry in Illinois. We'd gotten some serious death threats on a campaign and packing it seemed — to quote the first of the two failed Bush presidents — prudent at the time. But that was a little too much drama for what I was planning to do.

I got out of my car and stretched. In case anybody was watching, I would look like just another weary traveler.

When I reached the door I saw that the metal frame had a small jagged piece sticking out. The rust on the edge of it showed that it had gone unrepaired. Getting in or out took some effort. I knocked. The traffic noise made it difficult to hear. I pushed my ear to the space between door and frame and knocked again. Still nothing.

I pressed the door with two fingers. It opened wide enough to let me pass through. I was pretty sure that whatever I would find inside would not make me happy.

Beer and marijuana were the dominant odors, thick enough to slice. Everything swam in muzzy darkness, the drapes closed. The TV set bolted high to the wall was on but the sound was turned off. Two arch actors performed a soap opera scene. On wire hangers in an open closet were three or four blouses and a dress. The stand between the beds was filled with used Bud cans. I walked over to them. One had a tiny roach on its top. In my day we'd eaten the roaches. Roaches were the best part of smoking weed. Or so the myth had gone, anyway.

A large old-fashioned cardboard suitcase lay on the bed, coffee colored, tan stripes on either end. The edges were worn away. They had a gnawed look, as if rats had feasted on them.

In most motel rooms there are the spirits of lust and loneliness in the corners. If you listen carefully late at night, you can hear them. They speak to you. They'd told me many things over the years about others as well as myself.

I walked over to the small desk. The surface of it was covered with a plastic-like coating. Never mind that the blond desk wasn't worth saving. The coating had done its job. It had stopped the small pool of blood from leaking onto the floor.

In the bathroom I found traces of pink water in the white sink. In the waste can I found a balled-up motel towel. It was stained bloodred.

I went back to the bed and the suitcase. I'd been careful not to touch anything except the doorknob. I was tempted to open the suitcase. I took out my handkerchief and started to drag the case closer to me when somebody knocked on the door.

I didn't say anything. I heard my heart in my ears. Finally, in singsong, a Latina voice said: "Cleaning rooms. You want it done now?"

A voice I didn't own or control said: "No thanks. Later."

"Aw right."

I let my heartbeat slow before opening the suitcase. Inside I found a jumbled mess. I covered my hand with the handkerchief and started pulling things out to examine them. The clothes ran to two T-shirts, two sweat-shirts, two pairs of jockey shorts, two pairs of socks, a pair of jeans, and then a range of toiletries from toothpaste to razor blades to pocket combs to mouthwash. There were four paperbacks, Camus and Sartre and Kerouac and William Gibson. I pictured a college student, though the owner could be older, of course. Stuck in a corner was a business card. I brought it up to my face so I could read it in the bad light. I didn't like what I saw at all.

Larson-Davies was a group that special-ized in opposition research. Detective work using not smoking .45s and bourbon but newspaper files and the Internet. They were ruthless and very good. For most of us in political work, elections are a contact sport. There are no saints in our business, just degrees of sinners. The Larson-Davies group believed in mortal combat. When their oppo people go after the background of their opponents, they rarely fail to dig up at least a modest scandal — or something that can be spun in the media as a scandal. They have helped bring down two or three senators once considered unbeatable.

Beneath the logo on the card was the name Monica Davies. Like Greg Larson, she was a former gossip columnist. She made considerably more money outing politicians than she ever made outing action heroes.

I'd learned something by coming in here, but I wasn't sure what as yet. How did Susan Cooper tie into the blood and the shabby suitcase and the business card?

The door was difficult to close. I had to jerk it hard before I heard the lock click. I put my head down the way people do in a perp walk and headed to my rental car. The temptation was to run, but I forced myself to just move quickly. Only when I got behind the wheel did I look to see who might have seen me. The walk was empty. The cleaning cart was in front of an open door but there was no sign of the woman.

I started the car and drove away. I rolled the window halfway down. I needed the breeze to dry me off. Even the tops of my hands gleamed with sweat.

All the way back to campaign headquarters, my mind kept flashing on that splash of blood on the desk. And the bloody towel in the waste can.

CHAPTER 2

Earlier that morning, after an hour in the hotel gym and a light breakfast, I had driven over to the Reelect Susan Cooper headquarters in the business district of Aldyne. I'd picked up a rental car as soon as I got off the plane last night. I'd been here once before, but I wanted to spend some time seeing the downstate city of eighty thousand and I preferred to do it alone. When you've got a tour guide, your impressions end up being theirs as much as your own.

I was here because the man I'd put in charge of the campaign, Ben Weinberg, was having problems with his candidate. This was the only time in the eight years we'd worked together that he'd asked me for any real help. I had a sense of how unhappy Ben was when I swung the rental car behind the large one-story building that had previously been a warehouse but was now our campaign headquarters. He was leaning next to the back door and he was smoking a cigarette.

Ben had played fullback at Northwestern. He'd kept in reasonably good shape for a man who slept five hours a night, had two marriages in his past, dined mostly at McDonald's, and had tried every possible gimmick to quit smoking. Last week he'd told me that he'd been off the smokes for five weeks and felt that this time he was going to make it. He waved at me with a burning cigarette in his fingers.

The morning was clear and bright. It was just after seven-thirty. I walked over to him and said, "You want a pep talk?"

He smiled. "Nah. Wouldn't do any good, anyway, Dev. This thing is spooking me and I don't know what to do about it."

Ben is sartorially challenged. Even in the best of clothes he looks rumpled. And he looks happy about it. A big, smart man whose necktie is never cinched at the throat and whose suit coat is rarely seen. The face fits the form, a comfortable composite of kind brown eyes, a mouth quick to smile, and a nose that had been broken in a few bar fights. He's of the old school of consultants. He's not coiffed and polished and ready for sound bites. He started out working in school-board elections back in Winnetka. That was when he was first married and had twin daughters. Then he got involved in local politics and then state politics, and then he ended up asking me for a job. He was my most important employee. We had one major thing in common: Our obsession with the job had left us without wives. I ate at McDonald's a lot, too.

"I appreciate you coming down, Dev."

"I just hope I can help."

"You had dinner with Susan that one night in Chicago. She said she really enjoyed it. Maybe she'll tell you what's going on."

"Her stepmother's no help?"

"Natalie Cooper? The Dragon Lady? Not hardly. Most of the money comes from her and she doesn't let you forget it. She keeps threatening to fire me."

"Yeah. Natalie said something like that to me, too. About both of us. That's another reason I came down here. I figured things must be getting rough."

"It's getting a little tighter than we'd hoped, for one thing. You always said that Duffy was going to be a lot tougher than we thought he'd be. And you were right. And then with Susan . . ."

He flipped his cigarette into the air like a missile. We both watched it arc and then splash down on the concrete alley that ran alongside the building.

"I've got some coffee going," he said. "Let's go inside."

Just as he said that, a silver Aston Martin swung into the parking area behind the headquarters. A blond man waved at us as he pulled in and parked. I didn't recognize him until he was out of the car and walking toward us, one of those compact, handsome men who would look good modeling expensive suits. Like the gray one he was wearing. His name was David Manning and he was Susan's husband.

"I was on the way to the foundation and I thought I'd stop in and warn you, Ben." He said this with a hint of amusement in his voice. "Natalie's coming over here this morning. She wants to see the new commercials." When he reached us, he put out his hand to me and we shook. "Good to see you again, Dev."

Manning was one of those guys you shouldn't like but did despite yourself. He'd known Susan in college. His looks made him popular, something that compensated for his background as the son of an alcoholic mother who'd raised him mostly on welfare. He now worked for Natalie as the head of the Cooper Foundation, the nonprofit that her late husband had established to do many, many good works. From everything we'd been able to learn about Manning, he didn't have to work very hard. The heavy lifting was done by his staff. He was around to look good, be charming, and represent the foundation around the country. He gave good TV. He was Natalie's paid boy, so much so that he sided with her as often as he sided with his wife. The relationship between stepmother and daughter had always been combative. Manning's boyish blandness allowed him to calm them both down when the need arose. But he never forgot who handed him the check twice a month.

"Thanks for the warning," Ben said.

"I shouldn't have been so flip about it," Manning said, apparently feeling guilty for making a joke about Natalie. "She just wants to make sure we win, Ben. That's all."

I was trying to concentrate on the conversation, but just then I saw a hawk riding the air and looking magnificent as hell doing it. In my days as an investigator for army intelligence I'd spent some time in the Rockies working on two different cases. I'd started to envy birds, serene and self-possessed.

I dragged myself back to the conversation. "How's Susan?"

Manning shifted position. In terms of interrogation body language I could see that I'd made him uncomfortable. "Just very busy. And just can't shake that cold of hers."

"She has a cold, David? Since when?"

"Really? You haven't heard her sniffling, Ben?"

"Oh, that. I figured she was using cocaine."

Manning smiled. "Don't say that around any reporters. Duffy's trying to play up her past."

"The polling we've done, her past doesn't seem to matter all that much. Less than ten percent say it's a concern."

I said, "We're having a little trouble with her, David."

"Oh? Trouble?" And he shifted position once again.

"Ben tells me she disappears sometimes without telling anybody where to find her. And she's lost her edge a few times in debates and interviews." I tried not to sound confrontational. It wasn't easy. I'd learned that Manning was good at evading direct questions.

"She's had some problems and Natalie's aware of them. She'll probably ask you for a little advice about it, in fact."

"You're her husband, David." This time I

sounded angry and meant to.

"I'd rather let Natalie talk to you about it, Dev. And anyway —" He glanced longingly at his car, the golden chariot that would take him far from us and our questions. "Anyway, I need to get to the foundation. I hope it goes well with Natalie. Wyatt'll be with her. He's good at keeping her calm." Wyatt was her husband.

He had a nervous smile for each of us and then hurried to his car. We watched him go. He even gave us a wan little wave just before he backed out.

"I can't help it," Ben said. "I feel sorry for him."

"Yeah, me too," I said. "That's quite the family he married into."

"A soap opera that doesn't need any writers."

"Oh, God, I'd forgotten that one." A conservative columnist had written a piece about Natalie's various "difficulties" with the campaign consultants she'd used on Susan's first campaign. She'd gone through three different firms. He'd come up with the soap opera line and it was, unfortunately, a good one and a true one.

"Well, let's go inside and I'll rip up your innards with some coffee I made."

I'd had plenty of Ben's coffee in my time. He wasn't kidding.

CHAPTER 3

Within half an hour the headquarters was open for business. The front part of the building was for the public and was manned by volunteers. In the rear was a long, narrow office for paid staffers. If you've ever worked for a newspaper you know what a campaign office is like: phones, faxes, computers; men and women who are the modern-day version of camp followers. Only in this instance they're following campaigns. They're political junkies who get paid for their obsessions. Both parties have them; neither party could function without them.

The modern political campaign has gone high-tech, of course, but it still serves the old masters. On any given day a campaign manager and his staff deal with a long list of jobs — fund-raising, Web sites, direct mail, grassroots organizing, yard signs, writing speeches, interpreting polling, dealing with the press, endlessly revising the candidate's schedule, and trying to chase down any persistent rumors about the opposition, most of which turn out to be bullshit. There's a lot of disinformation coming from both camps, disinformation meant to confuse the other camp and make them waste time trying to make sense of it. Then there are the staff wars. Some groups gather for a particular campaign function smoothly, a real team. Others are warring factions that can seriously damage a campaign or even destroy it.

In the three hours I sat at my computer in Ben's office that morning, I saw nothing but professionals going about their jobs efficiently and cordially. This was a testament to Ben's judgment. He'd chosen his people carefully. I checked on the other campaigns my firm was working on. There didn't seem to be any serious problems with any of them. The only trouble was here with Susan Cooper's sudden, mysterious loss of interest in her campaign.

I spent some time up front, too, meeting the volunteers and getting their assessment of the campaign thus far. During the day the volunteers tended to be retired women and men. A new category had recently been added — the unemployed. With the economic disaster facing the country these people divided their time between looking for work and trying to help the candidate they thought had a genuine interest in helping them improve their situation.

I was just wrapping up a phone call with one of our people who was spending the day at the state capital when somebody peeked in the office door and said, "She's here!"

He made it sound as if we'd just been invaded. And he wasn't far from wrong.

CHAPTER 4

Natalie Dowd McConnell Cooper Byrnes was born in Chattanooga, Tennessee, on July 4, 1960. Despite the fact that she remarried after the death of her second husband, Senator John Cooper, she continued to use his last name. Her family had been prominent both before and after the Civil War and had moved easily into national politics. Her great-grandfather, her grandfather, and her father had all served as senators. Natalie Dowd was so much of an elegant beauty that a famous portraitist named Ralph Hodges fell in love with her in the course of painting her for the family's mansion wall. She'd been fifteen at the time, and Hodges forty-six. A rumor still persisted that they'd mated up. Natalie loved the attention. Not every Southern debutante found herself in the pages of *People* and *The National Enquirer*. Her father allegedly hired a man to murder Hodges but was dissuaded by his wife. Hadn't the family reputation suffered enough already?

Natalie went to New York City, where she performed in several off-Broadway plays. This was where she met and married Randy McConnell, an actor who was plucked from the stage to play a TV action hero in a series that would run for several years. He took Natalie along with him and they were married in Los Angeles. Four years to the day after their wedding vows, McConnell broke the nose of his male costar, accusing him of sleeping with Natalie. Nothing was ever proven, but the incident did bring Natalie back into the public eye and led to many TV acting jobs. She'd worked hard with a vocal coach and lost her accent entirely. With her killer looks and competent acting skills she was able to support herself quite well when McConnell finally sued her for divorce after finding her at a party in a gazebo with another family friend. McConnell didn't hold up well during all this. He went on three different talk shows pretty much snockered and hinted that his ex-wife was something of a tramp. Natalie's father immediately sued him for slander.

Having grown up in a politically conservative family, it was logical that she would gravitate toward conservative functions. She was invited six times to the George H. W. Bush White House, where she used her passable voice to sing Gershwin and Porter songs. One of those times, her series coming to an end, she decided to stay in Washington for a while. She became a regular on the social scene. The men lusted after her body; the women lusted after her throat. She dated liberals and conservatives alike as long as they were powerful and not handsome enough to overshadow her when they were photographed together.

It was at one of these power parties that she met the recently widowed John Cooper. The local gossip columnists had immortalized this meeting, saying that when they first danced together people stood aside to watch them because they looked so perfect together. They were married soon enough. Though they spent most of their time in Washington, they kept their Aldyne mansion warm and cozy, hoping that his daughter, Susan, and his new wife would become friends. The two despised each other from the start and still do to this day.

A creature of Washington now, Natalie decided that she would lose some of her prestige if she was not represented by an elected family member. Her husband had died of a heart attack. Susan was going through her wild-child days. Natalie waited her out. Susan gave up drugs, drinking, and fornicating on car hoods. If this were a religious movie, you'd say she'd had a conversion of some sort. But as Susan insisted, it was just that she was sober enough for the first time in years to see what a spoiled and selfish bitch she'd become. She started working, and working seriously, in Chicago soup kitchens and inner-city hospitals. Though they rarely spoke, Natalie believed that Susan's work with the poor had made her a formidable candidate in this election cycle. Susan resisted at first but then began to see that maybe she could play a small role in helping the kind of people she'd worked with and truly loved. She agreed to run. A *Washington Post* reporter noted that "payback" for the money Natalie had put into the campaign was her right to drag the new congresswoman to every important party of the season. Susan even had to pretend that she liked Natalie.

I'd learned most of this on the Internet.

I walked up front preparing myself for all the smiley faces I'd have to make. Natalie had flown to Chicago with Susan four different times when we were outlining the reelection campaign. I had a lot to drink after each meeting. She usually brought

Susan's husband, David Manning, as well as her own husband, Wyatt Byrnes. They were easy to get along with. Dealing with Natalie made the idea of keeping a cyanide tablet under your tongue sound appealing.

She stood now in the glowing autumn light slanting through the tall front windows of the headquarters. She wore a tailored gray suit. The jacket had only one button so that it would emphasize the curves of her breasts and hips. She was as sexual an animal as she'd always been. And her breasts were her own — no store-boughts for her — and if she'd had any facial surgery, it was impossible to detect. The brown eyes gleamed with the same intensity as the dark shoulder-length hair. She was Scarlett O'Hara, but in this version she got to keep the family manse. I remember waking up one morning and realizing that I'd had a fantasy about sleeping with her. A novelty: sleeping with a woman you despise. The mindless perversity of lust.

"Now, there's a handsome man," she said.

"How are you, Natalie?" I said.

"I didn't sleep well last night. Worrying about the campaign. I'm sure I look it this morning."

"She just wants a compliment. She knows she's gorgeous." On the other side of her,

Wyatt Byrnes nodded a silent greeting to me after quick-drawing his compliment about her indisputable gorgeousness. There was something Western about him, the cut of his gray suit, the tanned good looks of a movie cowboy, and the spare manner of speaking and moving. Randolph Scott, maybe. When he watched her, as now, there was usually amusement in the brown eyes, as if he'd married a phenomenon as much as a woman. She seemed to entertain him. He didn't seem to mind that she was still known as Natalie *Cooper.*

Ben walked up next to me. He had told me that Natalie had been particularly tough on him the past week. She phoned him three, sometimes four times a day with "suggestions." Natalie's interference was taking its toll on him.

"Ben, did you set up that editorial meeting I phoned you about?" Her voice was sharp, her gaze even sharper when she addressed him. No amenities.

"Natalie, we've already met with their editorial board."

"Yes, and I told you that I listened to the tape and I wasn't happy with what you had Susan say."

I could feel Ben tense up. His hands were fists. Natalie had the money and thus the authority. Ben had the brains and the track record. But money trumped everything else, and he was getting that sad fact rubbed in his face right now.

"I didn't have her say anything, Natalie. She told them what she believed."

"Well, you're the campaign manager. You should have told her not to say that she favored decriminalizing marijuana and that she still won't vote for the death penalty. That radio bastard read her the murder statistics in Chicago and she still came out against it. And the station made that their lead when they endorsed Duffy, how he believed we should start executing people again in this state. All she needed to say was that she was looking at the issue again." Then, "And where is she, by the way?" Natalie snapped, glancing around as if Ben might be hiding her somewhere.

I could see she was ready to go at Ben again, so I said, "Why don't we look at the two new television commercials, Natalie? We have them ready to go in the office back there. I'm pretty sure you're going to like these."

Before she could speak, Wyatt Byrnes said, "That sounds like a fine idea, Dev. Let's have a look at them."

His wife didn't look happy that he had

interrupted what was probably another tirade. She frowned at him but then sighed. "These had better be much better than the last ones."

I risked a quick smile at Ben.

Ladies and gentlemen, the one, the only, Natalie Cooper.

CHAPTER 5

Give a cable news talking head five minutes to bitch about politics today and he or she will likely mention the process consultants use to bring their wares to market. Focus groups seem to bother them especially. I've never understood why. A cross section of twelve people studying commercials and print ads can often point out flaws that the consultants miss. This doesn't mean that you find every comment useful. Some of them can get pretty dumb. But most focus groups produce at least one or two insights that are worth discussing later on.

The two thirty-second spots I showed Natalie that morning had been produced, tested, reshot, and then tested again. The first focus group, which leaned toward the moderately conservative, complained that when Susan spoke about helping people, the ads sounded as if she was just another big-spending liberal. In this part of the state conservatives won three out of four elections. We retooled.

The new spots showed Susan in a factory, on a farm, in an office building, talking to people with jobs. The word "hardworking" could be heard three times per spot. We needed to make it clear that while Susan was pushing for extended unemployment benefits and help for the needy, she had a great respect for average people still working their asses off five or six days a week. Conservatives never seem to understand that people collecting unemployment have usually paid for it from payroll taxes. Or that there really are people who would die without state or federal aid.

Kristin Daly, Ben's number two, offered Natalie and Wyatt coffee and seated them in front of a big-screen TV, a black DVD player squatting on top like a parasite that drew power from all the electricity. They both declined the coffee.

By now Ben was sweating. The fluorescents gave the gleam on his face a ceramic glaze as he inserted the DVD. I don't sweat much. I grind my teeth instead.

Just before the commercials ran, a woman of maybe thirty came in with David Manning. Walking in front of several people seemed to be an ordeal for her. She kept her head down and walked in quick, anxious little steps. In her inexpensive beige suit she was thin and prim and out of place here in this room filled with power and anger and harsh competence. She was pretty in a shy, almost sad way. Manning introduced her to Ben, Kristin, and me as his assistant, Doris Kelly. She managed a tiny nervous smile for us. Judging by Natalie's laser-eyed glare, I was sure she didn't approve of the Kelly woman. Wyatt Byrnes gave her a little salute. Natalie did not look pleased. Byrnes was so cordial most of the time it was difficult to imagine him in a boardroom of business thieves and pirates.

Ben, Kristin, and I didn't watch the commercials. We studied Natalie's face. Being an actress, she knew how to conceal her feelings. When the second spot ended and the screen went black she sat back in her chair as if giving the new commercials thoughtful consideration. Then she said, tossing it off, "Well, that's an improvement anyway."

Like most slave owners, Natalie had learned that giving real praise only encouraged laziness among the creatures who did your bidding. I had never heard her give anybody in my firm an honest compliment.

"Much better, I think, Natalie." Byrnes

gave me a nod and a hollow smile.

Manning said, "I think you folks nailed it this time."

Doris Kelly offered no opinion. She was no doubt afraid to.

If Natalie hadn't given her reluctant approval of the commercials, Byrnes and Manning would either have said nothing or expressed mild disappointment. They'd been trained to wait for Natalie to tell them what their opinion was.

She looked at me. "I want another shot at that Gil Hawkins radio show. Ben doesn't think it's important, but I do. I want her to go back on there and tell that man's audience that she'll at least reconsider reinstituting capital punishment in this state. Obviously she can't vote in the state legislature, but she needs to make herself clear that she might vote for it if she could. And I've been thinking about the marijuana thing. What she should've said was that we might be forced to legalize certain small amounts of marijuana because the police are so overworked that they should be concentrating on more serious crimes."

Manning's eyes showed tension, Doris Kelly's misery, and Byrnes's a hint of amusement. He was like the little kid you knew in second grade who wanted to see what would happen when you rode your bike off the roof of the garage.

"We can try to get her back on the show," Kristin said. "But first of all I wonder if it's a good place for us. You have a hostile host and pretty much of a Limbaugh audience. I don't think we're going to make a hell of a lot of converts there."

"He's got the best afternoon numbers of anybody in the state. Or don't you people read radio ratings?" She turned her angry voice on Ben. "I expected you to prepare her better. But as usual you let me down."

I knew he wasn't going to put up with it anymore. I shut up and let him talk. The way he was hunched over, you could see he was thinking of throwing a punch. Not at her but maybe at the wall. And the way his breath was seething forth from his nostrils made me think of an animal waiting to charge. But he knew the game, and he'd been slapped around by the best and the worst of them, as had most of us, so he managed to sound almost civil when he spoke. "Natalie, the night before the interview I took Susan out to dinner. And for one solid hour that's all we talked about. The show. And how she should handle herself. And what she should say when one of his fascists called in and accused her of

46

being a communist or a whore from her old days. I even had a list of likely topics for her. And we went over them one by one. Capital punishment and legalized marijuana were right up there with taxes and war. I gave her my suggestions on how she should talk about them. Just kind of shave them a little bit so that he wouldn't jump on her. But she said, and I quote, 'Fuck him. These are two things I really believe in and I'm not going to kiss his ass.' I went with her to the studio and on the drive over we went down the list again. I suggested one more time that maybe we could go easy on these two particular subjects, but she went through the 'Fuck him' routine again. Now, if you want to take it up with your stepdaughter, that's fine with me. But I'd appreciate it if you'd quit telling me that I'm not doing my job."

Most people would have apologized, said, "Hey, I didn't know any of this and I'm sorry I jumped on your back." But this was Natalie Cooper.

"You're paid to handle her."

"Not *man*handle her, I'm not."

Byrnes said gently, "Come on, Natalie. They're serving panfried trout at the club this afternoon." He smiled at Ben.

Natalie stood up. I made the mistake of

thinking it was over. But Natalie frequently had a surprise ready. She took two steps toward Doris Kelly, hovered over the small woman where she sat, and said, "I'm not quite sure what you're doing here, Doris."

There was no way Doris was going to defend herself, so Manning, getting awkwardly to his feet said, "I invited her, Natalie. We handle a lot of things at the foundation for your campaign. I thought she might like to visit the headquarters here and see how things are done."

"I'm more interested in her seeing how things are done at the foundation, David. She's not exactly the best secretary you've ever had."

A noise that might have been a sob caught in Doris's throat. She looked as if she'd just been stabbed — and in a way, she had.

"Oh, for Christ's sake, Doris," Natalie said. "I didn't mean for you to get all upset. I've already talked to you about being a little more outgoing. You're not only David's secretary, you're also the receptionist. Your secretarial work is satisfactory, but you need to work on greeting people. You're so damned shy. Now, don't make a big production out of this. You'll just look like a fool."

Then she was gone.

CHAPTER 6

Susan Cooper stood in the doorway as if she wasn't sure she should come in. "Hello, everybody. Sorry I missed the morning meeting."

The only person who spoke to her was Ben. "You look like you're scared to come in. C'mon, for God's sake."

As she entered, her gaze swept the office and the eight people working at their desks. "I'm sure you're pissed off at me, so let me apologize for being late. But the important thing is, I'm ready now for anything we need to do."

As lovely and stylish as she was — and despite the fact that she was the client — she didn't have the authority Natalie did.

She tossed smiles like flowers until her eyes settled on me. The gray gaze narrowed and the smile pursed. She wasn't happy to see me because my presence told her that Ben had sent for me because he was having problems with her.

"Hi there, Dev."

"Morning, Susan."

"I'm sort of surprised you're here. I mean, I thought you were working on the Michigan campaign." Her look strayed to Ben as she spoke. There was a tone of accusation in her voice now.

"Michigan's going fine. I like to drop in on our campaigns and see how things are going. You know, firsthand, one-hundred-thousand-mile checkup."

"Well," she said as she walked across to the coffeepot, her long legs perfect in shape and tone. Her ankles could break your heart. "I read the internals every day." She poured herself a cup, then turned around and faced me. "It's tightening up a little, but we expected that." Then, "By the way, Peter — you know, my stepbrother — he's very unhappy that you're not using any of the speeches he's writing."

"He's a terrible writer, Susan, you know that."

"Oh, I forgot. You two had a little disagreement about that."

Peter Cooper was a failed politician. He'd run for Congress in this district but lost. He was terrible on the stump and worse on TV — nervous, irritable. He resented the fact that Natalie browbeat Susan into running for the same seat years later. She'd won and he hated her for it. His job was running her constituent services office and he was damned good at it. Every once in a while he'd write speeches and send them to Ben. He got pissed that Ben bounced them all, so he started bombarding me with them. We'd had sharp words.

"I'll talk to him about it," Kristin said. "It's my turn."

Susan frowned at me. "You didn't look as if you agreed when I said things were tightening up but that we were doing all right."

"He's coming on strong, Susan," I said, "very strong."

"What's that supposed to mean?" Her words were sharp enough to get everybody's attention. Now they were all watching us, her leaning against the coffee bar, me sitting on the desk chair I'd just turned around to face her. This was better than TV. The boss and the client getting into it.

I walked over next to her so that I didn't have to raise my voice. As I refilled my cup I said, "It means just what I said, that he's coming on strong. Which means we have to come on strong."

We were having two conversations, the one

everyone could hear and the unspoken one, the latter being about her not staying focused, not fighting hard enough.

"His side has a lot more registered voters than ours does, Susan. And we have to remember that."

She turned that chic face on the staffers and said, "I appreciate all you're doing for me. I've had some personal things I've had to attend to. But they're being handled now, and I promise you I'm going to start kicking ass again."

A few of them laughed. She was a hard worker and a no-bullshit boss. She didn't play any games and she was generous with her people. We knew this because we always talk with the client's staffers to get some kind of fix on who we'll be working with. Some clients resent this. Susan was happy we were doing it.

"And to prove it I'm going to humiliate Steve Duffy in the next debate. I was too nice the last time. This time I'm going to slap that fratboy smirk off his face."

I was smiling with the rest of them. Ben high-fived me. Susan had good instincts. She knew why I was here, and she was going to shut me down fast so that I'd hop on that plane and head back to Chicago. "Could I see the internals, Ben?"

Then it was back to work. I finished up my e-mailing while Susan and Ben went over our own tracking polls. These polls weren't as simple as how many points we were up and down. They detailed how we were doing with various groups broken down by income, education, ethnicity, religion, and address. I'd looked them over a half hour ago. I was still unhappy with the blue-collar vote. Though we were nine points ahead of Duffy right now, in economic times like these we should have been hitting fourteen, fifteen points ahead. But Duffy's days as a sportscaster — and not a loudmouth, either; a good, solid pro who knew what he was talking about — gave him an edge with males across the board.

After going over the internals, Susan and Ben talked about the scheduled radio interview she'd be doing this afternoon. This interview would be different from the one she had done with Gil Hawkins. He hated her politics and had done everything he could to make her look bad. Don Stern was a real reporter. His questions this afternoon would be tough but fair.

Like most politicians, running for reelection meant stealing days from her duties in Washington. Generally she'd fly home for weekends and the weekends were packed with speeches, events, interviews. For example, when she finished with the radio interview, she'd be attending a women's business conference. She was the keynote speaker at this conference, which started on a Friday afternoon. It was a regional gathering of successful businesswomen. Duffy would be speaking tomorrow. There would be a lot of press. We needed to make a good showing.

"A friend of mine is in the hospital here, Ben. I want to run over there and spend an hour with her if I can. The interview isn't till one, so I'll have plenty of time to just meet you at the radio station."

"I was hoping we'd have lunch together and go over a few more things, Susan."

"There'll be plenty of time for that tonight." A studied laugh. "Don't worry, Ben. I'm not going to wander off again."

"Think I'll head down the hall," I said. "I'll be back in a few minutes."

When I left, Susan was still trying to reassure Ben that he could trust her again. They were so busy talking that they didn't notice that I'd grabbed my topcoat on my supposed trip to the men's room. I went out the back door, slid under the wheel, and backed a quarter of the way down the alley. There was a narrow spot in front of a loading dock where I could hide. Susan didn't know what my rental looked like, and as far as she was concerned, I'd just made a trip to the john, nothing more suspicious.

She didn't emerge for another fifteen minutes. She'd probably spent the time showing off the shiny, fine, trustworthy Susan to the staffers. She hesitated before opening the door of her new green Volvo. She took a deep breath. Her blond hair gleamed in the sunlight. Then she eased herself into the car and left the parking lot. I gave her a half-block head start. I'd done a fair share of tailing in my army intelligence days. I hoped I hadn't lost the touch.

At the time I had no idea where she'd be leading me. My first shock was seeing the shabbiness of the motel. The second was seeing her rush from the room as if she'd witnessed something terrible. The third was going into the room myself and finding the bloody towel in the bathroom.

The new, improved, trustworthy Susan wasn't any of these things at all.

CHAPTER 7

On the way back from following Susan, I called Ben on my cell and asked him if he'd seen anybody from the Larson-Davies oppo research group in town here.

"Oh, yeah. Monica and Greg Larson himself. The *Chronicle* is doing profiles of state political people who went on to become national. Since Monica and Larson are working for Duffy, the *Chronicle* had them come here for photos, you know, his hometown and all. Why, you thinking of asking her out again?"

"Don't remind me."

Several years earlier, in a zombie state following my divorce, I ended up in the arms, if not the bed, of Monica Davies. We missed the bed part because we were both so drunk we passed out on her hotel room couch. Just before we were to stagger into bed she brought out a joint the size of a finger and it made us both comatose within ten minutes. This had been in Vegas at a convention for political soldiers. Hard to say who was more disgusted — me for betraying my side or her for betraying hers. The few times we'd met since then we'd been resolutely cold.

"Any particular reason you're asking?"

I could have told him about her business card being in the cheap suitcase I'd found in the motel room, but I decided against it for now. "Somebody said they thought they saw her in a restaurant here. I was just curious."

"Yeah, in fact I ran into Larson the other night at a bar where the local reporters drink. He was telling them all his war stories and they were eating it up. According to him, everybody on our side is a traitor, a terrorist, and a sexual deviant who would put de Sade to shame."

"Good old Greg."

"Hey, are you insinuating he'd lie?"

"Of course not. Not our Greg."

The only hotel in town with four stars was where I happened to be staying, the Commodore. If they were in town it was likely they were staying there also. I could double up lunch with finding out if they were under the same roof.

For lunch I had a BLT and a glass of

ginger ale and then I went looking for them. Detective work should always be this easy. She was in room 608 and he was in room 624.

I stepped off the elevator to find a bellhop leaning against the wall talking fast into a cell phone. He looked and sounded agitated. I'd spent a year reading Jim Thompson novels set in hotels that were actually concentration camps of sorts. This guy looked like he'd fit in there.

He dropped his voice when he saw me emerge but not so low that I couldn't hear him: "So I made a mistake. How many times do I have to say I'm sorry?" He clicked off, stuffed the phone in the pocket of his gray-trimmed blue uniform. He was in his thirties, chunky, balding. He had one of those put-upon faces that not even a smile would light up. "Help you with something?" he said.

"Just looking for room 608."

"Right down here, sir." He pointed to his left. The corridor was carpeted in dark brown to complement the tan walls and brown trim. The wide window at the end of the corridor gleamed with thin autumn sunlight. He walked down to the room and stood beside it like somebody in a print ad pointing out a product.

I knocked. He started walking back toward the elevator. I knocked again. This time of day the sixth floor was quiet except for elevator doors opening and closing. I knew nobody was going to be answering here. I saw the bellhop starting to get on the car and I said: "Could I talk to you a minute?"

He turned around and shrugged. "Sure."

"The woman in room 608. Do you know who I mean?"

"The Davies woman."

"Have you seen her around today?"

He bit the inside of his lip and looked past me. His mind was still on the phone. "Today? I don't think so."

"I need to talk to her about something. I've had a hard time reaching her."

He was suspicious. "So you know her, you mean?"

"We work for the same company. I was supposed to meet her for lunch. I just got in about three hours ago. But she didn't show up."

"Oh."

"One of our men might have been around here, too. Did she have any visitors that you know of?"

"You mean Mr. Larson? He's staying right down the hall. He sees her two, three times a day."

"Anybody else ever see her?"

He just stared at me and said, "Did I mention that Mr. Larson is a good tipper? You must know him. She told me that he's her partner in some kind of political firm."

I reached for my wallet. I gave him a ten.

"You kidding, man? You know the kind of shit this place would give me for even talking to you about stuff like this?"

I gave him a second ten.

He stuffed the bills into the same pocket the cell phone rode in and said, "One guy. Big redheaded guy. Expensive suit. Gold watch. But there was something rough about him. You've seen guys like him. No matter how well they dress they still come across as rough."

"How many times have you seen him?"

"At least three times in the past two days. Last time they had a real argument. Bad enough that somebody called down to the desk about it. I came up. He was in the doorway when I got here. He was still arguing, but when he saw me he left right away. Damned near knocked me down getting out of here. She was standing there looking really pissed at him. She slammed the door in my face."

"You ever hear her call him by name?"

"Oh, yeah, she called him a name all right.

A couple of them. 'Piece of shit' and 'bastard.' Once she even got him with 'motherfucker.' "

"So no ID on him at all?"

"No."

I took out my card and gave it to him. I scribbled the number of my cell phone on it. "There's another twenty in it for you if you call me when you see her next time. Call me right away."

"So you work with her, huh?" He smirked. "The hell you do."

"All right, thirty if you call me."

"I'm working through the dinner shift tonight. I need to buy my lady a nice gift. I had a little fun with one of the girls who work in the kitchen and she took it serious. Called the apartment for me where I live with my lady. I've been trying to tell her it didn't mean anything — my lady, I mean. You know, a little nookie on the side? She's making a big thing out of it." He grinned. Not smiled, grinned. He was presenting himself as a man of the world and happy with his self-image. The nudge as ass-bandit.

"That's a tough act to sell. That it didn't mean anything." I was thinking of my own ruined marriage. It had meant something to my wife when I'd betrayed her and it had

meant something to me when she'd betrayed me.

"She'll come around. Especially if I can hit you up for ten more right here."

"Yeah, and what's that going to get me?"

"I could always forget to call you when Ms. Davies shows up."

There were at least three radios going in headquarters when I got there. Small groups had gathered around each. A few of the more ardent listeners were using their bod-ies as well as their mouths to show support. They'd bob and weave like fighters when the host asked something they didn't like and they'd victory-jab their arms in the air when Susan scored a particularly telling point. But the on-air atmosphere was friendly. Don Stern's questions were on point but not malicious. Unlike radio assas-sin Gil Hawkins, who'd done everything he could to humiliate Susan, Stern genuinely wanted to know where she stood on issues and how she felt about her two terms in Congress.

I stayed for ten minutes. The questions I heard dealt with the economy. Jobs and mortgages. Susan was prepared, smooth, and confident. I admired her ability to put aside what had happened in the motel room earlier.

Ben and Kristin had their own radio going in the office. I slid into a chair and listened.

STERN: But you've been in Washington for two terms, Congresswoman Cooper, so aren't you at least partly responsible for the fix we're in?

SUSAN: Don, you're right, I've been there for two terms. But if you look at the facts, in my first term I demanded that we look into some of the more obvious dishonest — if not illegal — practices on Wall Street. There were a number of us who saw what was going to happen long before it did.

STERN: Well, that's true, but you were never able to get anybody to support you. I mean you couldn't get the head of the House Banking Committee to support you — and he's a member of your own party.

SUSAN: Yes, and I talked to him about it several times.

STERN: By "talk," do you mean argue?

SUSAN: *(laughs)* I'll use *my* word. "Talked."

STERN: Well, to play devil's advocate

here, Congresswoman Cooper — you're asking the voters to reelect you because of your experience. But what good is experience if you can't get anything done?

SUSAN: Don?

STERN: Yes?

SUSAN: Would you say that the *Chronicle* is a conservative newspaper?

STERN: It's not as conservative as it used to be.

SUSAN: *(laughs)* Thank God for that. But you'd still agree that it's a conservative newspaper by and large. Especially the editorial page.

STERN: *(laughs)* I don't know where you're going with this, but I'm happy to listen.

SUSAN: Where I'm going, Don, is that you still quote it frequently. But the one thing you haven't quoted is their editorial last week about me being the most effective House member of the Illinois delegation. So doesn't that make it sound as if my experience has been paying off?

The rest of the ninety minutes went well, too. A few of the callers were harsh. They were obviously for the other side. But she handled them easily and with humor whenever that seemed appropriate. Even more impressive, she was a human computer when it came to facts and figures and the intricacies of Washington. Stern complimented her a few times for her grasp of subjects. Our opponent was good on his feet, too, but not as good as Susan Cooper.

Toward the end of the show Kristin started talking about this new cocktail dress she was going to wear tonight to the fund-raiser downtown. Kristin was a vivid redhead of thirty. I'd hired her because of her background in planning events for large hotels. Political events can unravel if they're not planned well and overseen with steely diligence. You're always up against places that don't care about your client the way you do. Right now Kristin was prom-night excited. All Ben had to say was: "I hope there are some single women there. It's been a long time for me."

"Gee, that's a good approach," Kristin laughed. "Be sure to mention you haven't had sex for a couple of years."

"See the kind of bullshit I have to put up with?"

Kristin smiled at me.

"Well, I guess I'd have to agree with Kristin on that one. I wouldn't mention that you haven't been with a woman until you're at least on your fourth drink."

"Or sixth," Kristin said. "You know, when she can barely hear anything anyway."

I stayed around to go over some fresh internal polling. Ben was disappointed we'd only gained back 1.5 percent of the previous internal dealing with blue-collar voters in the northernmost edge of our voting district. Kristin thought we were trending up and should be happy. Then Ben wanted to talk about bringing a senator into the district to campaign with Susan. He was hoping for a man I respected but who was given to saying the wrong thing at key moments. You had to exorcise him before you put him up on the platform or the demons would take him over. We decided to ask a safer if slightly dull choice who had a good relationship with unions. He had never been known to make a joke about his opponent's rather large nose.

When I got to the door, I said, "I may see you tonight. Right now I need to do a couple of things."

I spent ten minutes up front with the volunteers, getting their read on the day. Everybody was still high-fiving. And hugging. And beaming. Susan had done very well indeed. I did a bit of acting, slapping hands and backs with a few of them I knew. And then I was outside in the melancholy autumn dusk that was a perfect match for my mood.

CHAPTER 8

I pulled up in my former spot at the Family Inn. A couple was unloading an SUV. A baby sat in her car seat crying. The couple took turns trying to calm her down as they trekked back and forth to their room. The door I wanted was four slots away. I knocked, waited. The lights of tall buildings and towers pierced the gray haze covering the half-moon. The McDonald's across the way was crowded. The drive-through had two long lines going. The baby continued to wail. I knocked again.

The door opened about an inch. She had to jerk it open because of the swollen frame. "Who is it?" A female voice, young.

"My name is Dev Conrad. I'd like to talk to you if I could."

"I'm not supposed to talk to anybody. Please just go away." Her fear made her sound even younger.

The door started to close. I risked shoving

my hand between it and the frame. I was pretty sure she wouldn't slam it on my fingers.

"Maybe I can help you."

"Please. Don't get me in trouble. We don't need any more trouble."

"I was in this room earlier. I saw the blood."

From inside I heard the sound of a TV newscast turned low. At the far end of the lot a pickup truck blaring country music pulled in. "Are you alone in there?"

After a pause: "Yes."

"You'd feel better if you had somebody to talk to."

"I don't know who you are."

"Somebody who wants to help you. And maybe you can help me."

"I'm not sure —" Then: "Oh, God."

She rushed off making sounds that I remembered from early in my marriage. My wife was sick a lot during her pregnancy with our daughter. We used to joke that she should just take up residence in the bathroom. I couldn't be sure that this woman was going through the same thing, but that was my first impression.

She hadn't bothered to close the door. I gave the door a shove and walked in. I flipped on the light switch. The bulb was dim, the light itself dirty yellow.

The cheap suitcase was still on the same bed. The other bed was messy from sleep. The first thing I did was go over to the desk. The cleaning had been crude but had gotten rid of most of the blood if you didn't look closely. There was a residue of cleaning solution on the desktop now. Amateur job. The cleaning woman would have had a more formidable solvent and she wouldn't have left traces of her work.

The vomiting started behind the closed bathroom door. I went over and sat down on the desk chair. On the screen starving children in Africa looked out at me in confusion and despair. When I took over the world I was going to kick a lot of ass. A whole lot.

Water ran in the sink. An electric toothbrush clicked on. When the nagging motor of the toothbrush clicked off she started to gargle.

When she emerged from the bathroom she looked no older than fourteen or fifteen, one of those waifs who is often painted with butterflies and rainbows all around them, out of a Victorian children's story. She was lovely in a pale anxious way. It was the kind of sorrowful appeal that brought out the protectiveness in men. Doubly so in her case because in addition to her jeans she wore a light-blue maternity smock.

"That's the only part of it I really hate. Barfing all the time. It makes me feel guilty, though. I shouldn't complain about it. We're actually going to have a baby this time. The last one — we lost it at four months."

"I'm sorry."

"Yes, so were we." Then: "You really shouldn't be here. You'd better leave."

"Who cleaned up the blood?"

"I did. But I didn't do a very good job, did I? I was really sick the last few hours."

"Whose blood was it?"

She walked over to the mussed bed and sat on the front edge of it. She put tiny frail hands together and placed them in her lap. She had a pink barrette in her long golden hair. It only emphasized the impression of her being very young. But now that I saw her more closely I saw a spent quality to her mouth and eyes that suggested she was probably in her early twenties. She looked at me and said, "I would really appreciate it if you'd leave. Bobby has everything under control now, so there's nothing you need to know anyway."

"That easy, huh? Bobby taking care of it?"

"Don't make fun of Bobby. I love him. He's a good husband."

"I'm not making fun of him, but if he's taken care of it, why are you so upset?"

She raised her head, taking the dusty air of the room deep into her lungs. When she fixed on me again she said, "This man came and —" She stopped talking and pressed her splayed fingers across her belly. "That's how I lost the first baby. I'm sure it is. All the stress we were going through. I don't want to lose this one."

"I want to help you. I don't like to see you like this."

"People are always saying bad things about Bobby. They don't understand that he's a good person."

She started to cry. Put one of those fragile hands to her face and wept. She kept the other hand on her belly, as if to reassure the infant inside.

I went over and sat next to her on the bed and put my arm around her. She didn't resist. I'd done this a few times with my own daughter, especially in her teen years. She leaned against me. "It's just so hard sometimes. And sometimes I think it'll never be any easier."

"You have to tell me what you're talking about."

"But if I do, he'll think I'm betraying him. He always says that about people. And he's right. But I don't have anybody else to talk to about it. I'm just cooped up here all the time."

"You can talk to me."

"I don't even know you."

"You said you need to talk to somebody. I'm trying to be your friend."

She dragged the palms of her hands down her gleaming face and snuffled up her tears. "Oh, God. You really should leave."

I waited a minute before I spoke. She had put her hands on the horizon of her belly and was staring at the wall.

"You're in trouble. Maybe I can help you."

The sigh was ragged. "It's just everything he tries — it never comes out right."

"What never comes out right?"

She raised her head. "I just feel so sorry for him. And for our baby."

"You'll feel better if you talk about it."

"Oh, damn," she said. And started staring at the wall again. And then she said, "Maybe you're right. Maybe I'll feel better if I talk about it." When our eyes met this time she said, "Why did you come here?"

"I followed a woman here."

"A woman?"

"Her name is Susan Cooper."

"You know her?"

"Yes. Do you?"

She looked away. "It all looked like it was going to work out for a while. This band he was in got a good gig in Vegas, but then they dumped him. He'd been their lead singer for two years. Went behind his back and got somebody else."

If this had been a puzzle you'd have realized that she'd just contributed at least two major pieces. And a picture was beginning to emerge. Bobby was a musician and she'd hinted that while there'd been trouble they hadn't had anything to do with it. Giving a picture of the kind of people they knew. The kind whose visits left blood behind.

"Was he hurt today?"

She pulled her head back so she could see me. "Hurt?"

"The blood. Was that your husband's?"

She shook her head. "No, no. Bobby can take care of himself. It was —" A deep sigh. She smelled of tears and shampoo. "I really can't say anymore."

He was there then. He managed to slam the door back against the wall in what seemed a second. And then he was charging me with a fist ready to smash me in the face.

I got my elbow in front of my face to block his punch, rising to my feet as he attacked. He was a few inches shorter than my six-two and on the slim side. But the arms at the end of his T-shirt sleeves were muscular and he knew how to fight. He stepped to the side of me, forcing me to turn and throw myself off balance in the process. He managed to hit me hard just below my cheekbone. But he made the mistake of hurrying in to follow up, and I was able to smack him with a blunt right hand to stun him. I cut his lip. He fell back against the desk.

"Stop it, Bobby!" she shrieked. "Do you know that our baby can hear everything that's going on? Do you want to lose this one, too?"

Her words had a powerful and immediate effect on him. "Oh, shit, I'm sorry, Gwen. I'm sorry." His words were troubled by what I'd done to his lip. His arms dropped to his sides. Then he ran a hand through his dark curly hair.

I walked to the door and closed it from inside. My head hurt from where he'd hit me. I was glad we weren't throwing punches any longer.

I came back and said, "We need to talk."

He wiped the blood from his lower lip with the back of his hand. "Who is this jerk, Gwen?"

"I'm not sure, Bobby. But he didn't hurt me. He was nice."

"Nice. Right." To me: "You know, I could call the cops and get you in a lot of trouble." He had a spiky beard that gave his handsome features a diabolical look. That was the whole idea. He was a standard-issue rock star type. The losers looked about the same as the winners. But the winners wouldn't have to stay in motels like this one.

"Go ahead and call them. You want to use my cell phone?"

"You trying to be funny?"

"Bobby, calm down. This isn't good for me. Or the baby."

He made dramatic futile gestures with his hands and turned to face the wall. He pressed his forehead against it and stayed that way for a full minute. I glanced at Gwen. She just shook her head.

"Something happened here this morning, Bobby," I said. "I'm trying to find out what."

He came off the wall and said, "Nothing happened here."

"There was a lot of blood on the desk. Somebody got hurt."

"How the hell did you know that?"

"I came in here and saw it."

"Yeah? How'd you get in?"

"The door was ajar. I walked in."

He shoved his hands in the back pockets of his jeans and then closed his eyes and lifted his head to the ceiling. I recognized the move. James Dean in *Rebel Without a Cause.* Nice to know that Bobby's generation was still honoring him. "This is really bullshit."

"Maybe we should tell him, Bobby —"

"No!" He dropped the pose and crossed to Gwen. "Honey, we don't know who this jerk is. Or why he's so interested in everything. You want to see me go to prison?"

"Oh, God, Bobby, don't even say that."

"Then don't say we should tell him anything."

Right now I was invisible to them.

Bobby got down on his haunches and put his head on her lap. She stroked it the way she would a child's. Her eyes glistened with tears. Bobby spoke, the words muffled: "You have to stay with me on this, Gwennie. Otherwise I'm going to be in real trouble."

It might have been an act. Hard to say. Maybe he wasn't as tough as he thought and was using his wife as his mommy. Or maybe he had to keep her on his side and this moment of fear and sadness was his way of ensuring her loyalty.

He stood up and pulled down his T-shirt and hitched up his jeans. "Pack everything, honey. I've already checked us out."

"Checked us out? Where are we going? I

don't want to leave, Bobby." Obviously this grim room had become a kind of home to her. The prospect of leaving it scared her.

"A nicer place, honey. Much nicer."

"But we don't have the money."

"What did I say about not talking in front of him? I'll explain all this later. My suitcase is ready to go. You just get your stuff ready."

He turned to me. "So that's it, man. We're leaving and I don't want to see you following us."

"How're you going to stop me?"

"I could always shoot out your tires."

"God, Bobby, stop talking like that. And you'd better not have a gun. You promised you wouldn't get one, remember?"

To me he said, "Get out of here. Now."

Gwen sat with her hands on the swell of her belly. She was crying again, silently.

I took out one of my cards and wrote my cell phone number on the back. I walked over to her and dropped it in her lap.

"What the hell you think you're doing?"

"I'm letting her know how to get in touch with me."

"Let me see that." He reached down to grab it, but I got his wrist before he could pick it up.

"This is between your wife and me. She needs a friend." To Gwen I said: "If he tears the card up, just remember the name of my business. They'll put you in touch with me. That number is answered twenty-four hours a day. Same with my cell phone."

I let go of him. He didn't face me for a while. I think he was more embarrassed than hurt. I had made him look weak in front of his wife. I wouldn't have appreciated that, either.

"Oh, God, Bobby, this is not going the way you said it would."

"Just shut up. And I mean right now." Then he walked to her and kissed her on top of the head. "It'll be all right, Gwen. We just have to stay cool is all."

"Remember, Gwen. Night or day, I'm ready to help you."

"You always sniff around other men's wives?" Bobby said.

"Just when they have husbands like you."

When I reached the door I looked back at them. She was weeping again. He sat down next to her and took her to him. They'd changed roles. Now he was the adult and she was the child. He kept stroking her head and kissing her on the side of her face. He was like most of us, a person of parts, in his case a violent punk capable of great tenderness.

CHAPTER 9

This was probably as close to the Hollywood style of red carpet as a small Midwestern city was going to get. The guests at the fund-raiser were dressed in evening clothes, and as they trekked across the lobby to the ballroom door a variety of digital cameras and video cams noted their appearance. They carried themselves with an air of prosperity and importance. The men favored dinner jackets, and the women cocktail dresses. There were gorgeous women of several ages, from the young to the elderly. This wasn't the faction of our party where you would find schoolteachers and union members. These were the people with money and they were vital to Susan Cooper's campaign.

The ballroom had been decorated with a diamond-flashing disco ball in the ceiling like God's eye overseeing the foolishness of the mortals beneath. The tables with their brilliant white tablecloths looked like large lilies. On stage was a local band called Black Velvet Elvis. Right now they were doing some very fine Chuck Berry. The singer was tall, lean, rock-star handsome, and his bass guitarist was a very young, pretty girl who even from here resembled him. Later I got a glimpse of the drummer. Very young but the same resemblance to singer and guitarist. A family affair? Even though few people had been seated, four or five couples were already on the dance floor going at it.

On the right corner of the stage was a rostrum. Susan would be introduced from here and would give a brief speech. An enormous black-and-white photograph of her formed the backdrop.

The only person I recognized was Peter Cooper. He was obviously still pissed because I didn't use his speeches. He gave me one of those reluctant little waves you give the man who's about to dump offal on your lawn and then scooted in the direction of the bar.

I didn't see any of my people. I wondered why they were late. I was just about ready to call them when I saw Ben hurry into the lobby. He washed a hand across his face. He was sweating. He looked around anxiously. When he saw me he took a deep breath and hurried over.

"Are you all right?"

"Yeah. After I've had three or four drinks I will be, anyway."

I pulled him into the cloakroom. There would be reporters roaming the ballroom tonight. The program itself wouldn't be much in the way of a story, but given the number of drinks that would be drunk tonight, a loose tongue just might give them a piece of gossip worthy of a lead story. I kept my voice low. "What happened?"

Ben wiped his face with his handkerchief. He needed to pull himself together. "There was this guy." He shook his head. "I was talking to Susan, going over this list of people she had to make time for tonight. The heavy rollers. There was a knock on the office door and I went to it and there was this guy standing there. Susan had her back to me. She was studying the list. But when she turned around — I don't know how to describe it. I thought she was in shock or something. She just stared at him. And then he smiled at her. He scared her and he was enjoying it. All he said was, 'I'll talk to you later, babe.' *Babe.* I couldn't believe it. Who the hell calls Susan 'babe'?"

"Then what happened?"

"Then he left. Just like that."

"What was Susan doing?"

"Sitting down. She just went over to the green armchair and sort of collapsed into it. I asked her if she was all right and she said yes, but I could tell she wasn't. She looked miserable — and scared. Then Kristin came back and she had notes she wanted to go over with Susan, so they got to work. It took a few minutes for Susan to be able to focus. But finally she got herself together as she worked with Kristin and then she finished up with me."

"And that was it?"

"I wish. I told her I'd drive us to the hotel here. So we go outside — by this time it's pretty much dark — and as we're walking across the parking lot, there he is again."

"Same guy who knocked on the door?"

"Right. He just walks out of nowhere and stands in front of us. He doesn't look at me at all. Just stares at Susan. And then he says: 'I need a couple of minutes with you, Susan. Alone.' All she says is that she's in a hurry. She was lucky to even say that. I could tell she was in shock again. She grabbed my arm and damned near broke it, she was squeezing so hard. I told him to get out of our way and started for him. Then he said: 'Tell him about me, Susan. Tell him what I do to people.' Then she kind of came out of it. Out of the shock, I mean. She said, 'Ben, wait in the car, would you please?' I started to say hell no I wouldn't, but she shook her head and said that she'd be all right. She said, 'This is something personal, Ben. And I need to handle it.' So what could I do? I went over and got in my car. I kept watching them. I wanted to make sure he didn't hurt her, physically, I mean. He's a scary bastard."

"What's he look like?"

"Big, redheaded guy. Good-looking, I'll give him that. But he's rough. Everything about him is rough."

I thought of the bellhop's description of the man who'd visited Monica Davies. This was the same man who'd visited Susan in the campaign office and who had accosted her in the parking lot.

"What did she say when she got in the car?"

"Quote: 'I don't want to talk about it. It's personal, Ben, and I ask you to respect that.' Unquote."

A man came to the doorway and helped his wife out of her evening coat, ending my conversation with Ben. We all smiled at each other the way people do in commercials. Ben and I went back to the lobby, where we saw a small woman with a TV camera mounted on her shoulder and a sterile blond reporter interviewing an attractive older woman standing next to her attractive older husband. He seemed pleased that his wife would be on TV.

We went back into the ballroom. The tables were filling up. Black Velvet Elvis was doing a very nice arrangement of two Ricky Nelson songs. The front man could really sing.

Because this was Ben's territory he started table-hopping. He'd come to know the important people in district politics and he had to pay them their due. More TV toothpaste smiles.

I was just about to go over and get myself a glass of pop from the bar when somebody stumbled into me from behind. I turned to find Kristin there.

"Sorry, Dev. I tripped. I'm so upset I'm crazy." Her blue eyes were frantic. She nodded to the lobby. "We need to talk."

There were two more reporters in the lobby. Local TV. They were interviewing anybody they could grab because most of the attendees were hurrying inside. The formal ceremonies would start in less than ten minutes.

We found a shadowy corner next to a darkened gift shop.

"They have a little dressing room backstage. She's in there and she won't come out. She keeps telling me to go away."

So much for Susan's ability to stay focused no matter what was going on around her.

"Any chance she'll come out in a few minutes?"

"I asked her that three times now. She won't answer. She just says to go away. And I have to pretty much whisper when I talk to her. There are a lot of people around backstage. They'll pick up on everything if I talk any louder. And there's press here. They'll love this."

"How do we get backstage?"

"C'mon. I'll show you. I know a way without going through the ballroom."

The kitchen resembled a war zone. Shouting, bellowing. Men and women in various uniforms cooking, carrying trays, filling glasses, opening ovens, preparing salads, sampling soups, the enemy being a collective appetite that had to be fed and satisfied.

A door in the far wall led to three steps that ended on the cusp of backstage. Black Velvet Elvis was just starting on a Fats Domino song in front of the curtain. I looked for press. The only people I saw had big plastic badges strung over their necks.

They were with the campaign. But even so they weren't paid staff. I didn't trust them.

There were stand-up microphones, flats, long tables, chairs. Probably most of the business here would be conventions and conferences.

I said hello to a number of people as we walked slowly toward two doors near the back. One door read *Stage Crew* and the other said *Private.* Kristin knocked on the latter one. It was one of those apologetic little knocks.

She didn't get any answer.

I put my ear to the door, listened. What I heard was the wrong kind of silence.

"She's gone."

"What? No way, Dev."

It was my turn to knock. No surprise, no response.

I put my hand on the doorknob, twisted it, and pushed into the room. A long metal coatrack on wheels, two comfortable armchairs, a long dressing table with the standard bulbs around the circular mirror. The lights were off. The dressing room was empty.

"Oh, shit," Kristin said behind me.

I didn't see anybody backstage. Black Velvet Elvis was now on to Buddy Holly. Kristin had followed me out of the dressing room. She was on her cell phone asking Ben if Susan was by chance in the lobby. "He'll go check. And I'll go out front and keep looking."

At times like these, even though you like to think of yourself as a rational, sensible being, all the end-game fantasies start preying on your mind. Where was Susan? Maybe she was preparing her resignation speech, trying to beat the press to the revelation it would soon be sharing with the world. Might as well get it over with. Maybe sitting in a nearby bar right now scratching out her speech on note cards — she did everything on note cards — preparing herself for one final news release.

She came from the west end of the stage. I got on my cell and let Ben and Kristin know I'd found her. She was small against the back of the looming curtains. She had her head down, didn't see me until she was ten yards away. She looked composed but pale. "I suppose you were looking for me, Dev. And I suppose Kristin told you I wouldn't let her into the dressing room. That was silly. I owe her an apology." The smile was faked but fetching. "I just went out for some air and I didn't want company."

I watched her carefully. Anxiety played in

the gray gaze, but she managed to give the impression she was in control of herself.

"We just wanted to be sure you were all right."

She laughed. "I have one mother already, isn't that enough?"

I walked with her to the dressing room. The door was still open. She walked inside and started to close it. Black Velvet Elvis had stopped playing. Somebody was addressing the audience. Telling jokes that weren't getting great responses.

I got as far as saying, "Susan, we really need to —"

"I'll see you in a little while, Dev," she said. And closed the door.

I went back to the ballroom and grabbed myself a scotch on the rocks. Kristin took my hand and led me around to meet numerous people. This was a good time for socializing. People were drinking but not yet drunk. The band started playing again, this time a series of Stones songs. An elderly man in a gold lamé evening jacket took Kristin to the dance floor and started bumping and grinding as she pretended not to notice. Every once in a while, though, she'd look over at me and smile and give me a helpless little shrug. If this guy got any more enthusiastic he was going to end up in traction. Then I saw her frown suddenly and I wondered why.

As soon as I sensed somebody stepping up on my right side I knew what had caused Kristin to frown. Greg Larson had invaded our fund-raiser.

Like his partner Monica Davies, Larson had come out of the entertainment business. He'd started life as a studio publicist but found gossip to be more fun and much more profitable. He wrote a syndicated column known for its nastiness and was frequently seen on talk shows with updates on anything that involved stars and scandals. He'd married three different aging stars and had managed to cadge a fair amount of change from each divorce. Eight years ago he'd turned his love of gossip toward politics and set up his own opposition research firm. He had connections all over the world and this made him especially valuable to politicians. He hired the usual suspects to do the grunt work of sifting through newspapers and other documents to dig up their kind of scandals while he practiced the kind of assaults that divorce detectives once did.

There was a senatorial reelection campaign two years ago. A friend of mine was working with an Iraqi vet named Bill Potter who'd lost both of his legs in Baghdad.

Potter was ahead in the campaign until his opponent signed on with Larson. Larson did his usual job. Potter's father was a college professor who'd written a number of antiwar pieces. Potter's brother was gay. And Larson dug up a high-school photo of Potter grinning and smoking a joint and giving somebody the finger. Then he discovered that he had been treated for post-traumatic stress syndrome after his second tour in Iraq. Larson came up with a commercial he called "Family Values" — Potter's family — a pinko father, a queer brother, and a dope-smoking smart-ass who couldn't handle a couple of tours in Iraq without needing some psychological help. So he'd lost a couple of legs — he was still a whiner and a candy ass. It was ugly and it worked. Larson's man had started twenty points behind and ended up winning by nine points.

"Nice crowd."

"It was till you got here, Larson."

"Aw, still bitter about that commercial, are you?"

Larson had the look of a Wall Street CEO, one whose fleshy body needed a lot more time in the gym and a lot less time at the table. But he had the hard good looks and the silver-gray hair that kept him dominant even in the company of younger men —

younger men more ruthless than he was.

"Heard you were in town and just thought I'd stop by to say hello."

In idle moments I'd had many daydreams of smashing his face in. Back when I was in army intelligence and investigating the sins of various officers I frequently met Larson's type. They were usually West Pointers and they were convinced of their superiority based on little more than that they knew the secret handshake of that institution. Their weapon was the sneer. To question them was to challenge them as they had not been challenged since they'd graduated. They would always bring up West Point at the first opportunity and commiserate with me because I'd never had the privilege of attending there myself. Putting me in my place, of course. I'd had a lot of daydreams of smashing them in the face, too.

"You always wear a dinner jacket?"

"Believe it or not, I've got a dinner party to go to tonight. It'll be a little higher class than this, Conrad, but I have to admit I haven't seen any of your guests eating with their hands yet. So I'm impressed."

He hadn't stopped just to say hello. We'd had too many near fistfights for him to be comfortable. One night in Chicago I'd gone so far as to throw him up against a wall. We had both been pretty drunk. Both staffs had jumped between us, stopping the fun.

"You haven't seen Monica around here tonight, have you?"

"Monica? What the hell would she be doing here?"

For once he'd dropped his drollery. "There's something going on. I don't know what it is yet, but it's got me worried."

"Why would I care what happens to you and Monica?"

The smirk was back. "Because, old boy, your people may be involved in it, too."

But I was sick of him now and his game, whatever it was.

"Hold this," I said, pushing my empty glass into his hand and walking away quickly. It is small victories like this that make life worthwhile.

Around ten o'clock, after the dinner and the speeches, the band started playing again and Kristin forced me onto the dance floor. For fast songs I have invented a series of miniature movements that to the casual eye seem to be what you could call dancing. But if you look carefully you'll see that I'm actually standing in one place and cleverly using elbows and hips to fool any dance critics who might be looking on.

"C'mon, Dev, move around a little. Look at me."

I was looking at her, which was a pleasure. That cap of gorgeous red hair and the slash of grin and the lithe body moving sinuously to the music. Since I'm neither pretty nor sinuous, I kept on dancing the only way I knew how. Stiff middle-aged white man gets his groove on.

Neither of us could go for much longer than thirty seconds without looking to the center of the floor where Susan was dancing. A long line of men had queued up to be the congresswoman's brief partner. Each of them got about a fourth of the song. She could really dance. Apparently, all her nights in clubs had taught her well. The TV people loved it. So did the guests with digital cameras. As long as we could see her, we were happy. She wasn't going to wander off without giving me the talk I deserved, as to just what the hell was going on.

Susan had competition in the form of her stepmother. Natalie had an even longer line of beaus, and where Susan was dancing just for fun, Natalie was putting on a show. In her mauve cocktail dress, her dark hair and makeup flawless, she was one of those absolutely perfect middle-aged women gerontologists are awed by. She was here to show the younger ones how to do it.

The few times she and Wyatt danced together, the cameras rushed to make the moment immortal. They danced to the slower songs and with such grace I wondered if they hadn't taken ballroom lessons together; their steps and their physical attitude had that kind of drama and poise.

Natalie was no doubt pleased to see that the cameras had now shifted in her direction. She wouldn't get as much screen time as her stepdaughter, but at least she'd be on the tube.

When they finished dancing, Wyatt Byrnes stepped aside so that a group of women could surround Natalie and gush. Byrnes's gaze met mine and he walked over.

"Enjoying yourself, Dev?"

"Do I look as uncomfortable as you do?"

"You noticed, eh?" He laughed. "I like dancing with Natalie. That's the fun part. On one of the cruises we took we got into ballroom dancing."

"What's not the fun part?"

He leaned in and said softly, "The people. I'm not much for parties and things like that. I'd rather be home with a beer, watching Western movies. My father read them and watched them all the time. Westerns, I mean. I guess I picked it up from him."

The rich man with the taste of the common man. Hard to know if it was genuine. Political spouses and important relatives are trained to be good copy. When the press comes around, have a good story for them. And make that story something the largest number of people can identify with. And make it an "Aw" story, as in "Aw, that's so nice he's just a regular guy." You have to be careful of "Aw" stories because they can get out of control fast and sound contrived and unctuous. For instance, never have your guy say that his lifelong ambition is to work in a leper colony.

"For what it's worth, Dev, I think you people are doing a good job for Susan. I know that Natalie can get a little testy now and then, but when we're alone she admits that you're doing everything you can. The problem is Susan."

On the edge of the dance floor Natalie stood with her admirers. When she was a little girl she'd probably dreamed of being popular in this way, show-biz popular. But now she'd begun looking around, her smiles stage tricks and her attention wandering.

"I think she's looking for me," Byrnes said. "I need to go and rescue her. Nice to see you, Dev."

I had a fresh drink and listened to the

band for a time. They did a pair of Stones covers that were especially good. Then I needed a break. I was on my way to the men's room when my cell phone bleated. I stopped and answered it.

"Mr. Conrad?"

"Yes."

"This is Tommy Nickels." Whoever he was — and I didn't have a clue — he was excited about something. "From the hotel? You said to call you?"

"Oh, right, Tommy."

"Something happened in her room. I was carrying bags past her room and I heard her arguing with somebody. I couldn't stop because I was loaded down and this guy was in a hurry to get into his room. I had to spend a few minutes before I got him all set up. Then I got back to the Davies woman's door and there wasn't any sound."

"Maybe the other person left. Was it a man, by the way?"

"Oh, yeah, definitely a man."

I wasn't sure why he had called. Did he think this kind of information would get him more money?

"There was a security man up here checking on something, Mr. Conrad. So just for the hell of it I had him knock on her door and see if everything was all right. I mean she and the guy were really arguing when I heard them. He knocked, but he didn't get any answer. I wanted him to let me in, but he wouldn't do it until he got the night manager's approval. Which he ended up getting. And that was when he found her."

Somebody would have to teach Tommy how to write a news story. The lead was always the most important part and it was now obvious what that lead was going to be.

"Is she dead, Tommy?"

"Yeah. Whoever nailed her got her with this small brass statue we have in some of the rooms. Like I said, it's small, but if you use it like a weapon, it'll get the job done for you. So is this worth another twenty?"

"Yeah," I said, but I was too troubled by what he'd just told me to pay much attention.

CHAPTER 10

I drove over to the hotel where the three of us — Monica Davies, Greg Larson, and I — were staying. Given the hour, the crowd was sizable. The police had the entrance cordoned off. Two TV crews were interviewing men in the uniform blue sport coats worn by hotel employees. And the ghouls drank it all in. I call them ghouls with complete hypocrisy. I've been a ghoul many times myself. Proximity to death is exciting because it isn't us who are dead. It might scare us and make us sick — people burned to death can haunt you for a long time — but it makes us feel lucky, maybe even for a moment or two, immortal. We're alive and they're not.

I parked my car and took my place with my fellow ghouls.

The entrance to the hotel was wide and well-lit, with long windows stretching across the entire width of the front. Beyond the glass I could see guests standing in small groups, talking about the invasion of the police and emergency workers. This was a better-dressed collection of ghouls than the one I was with. A pair of uniforms burst out of the front door. The white box-style ambulance that had been parked on the front walk now went into reverse and got as close to the doors as it could.

She came down in a black body bag on a white gurney. Comments crackled through the crowd like summer thunder — flashes of pity, excitement, and even black humor. Not even professional wrestling could beat the death of a young woman. It was devoutly to be hoped that she'd been good-looking and nude when they'd found her.

The crowd on the far side of the rope line had the preferred view of the ambulance. They were mere feet from it. Several of them were pointing things out to one another as the ambulance team raised the gurney up and over. The first thing I noticed about the people over there was that two or three of them were attractive women. I'd never meet any of them, but glimpsing them was fun in a melancholy way. Then, behind the tallest of the women, standing next to the building in the cold autumn night was the red-haired man.

Tan Burberry coat, collar up, long red hair with a curl that touched his forehead. A blunt harsh face that was handsome in a severe way. You saw them in Chicago working for businesses that were secretly owned by the mob. They knew how to talk properly, dress properly, and be polite. They were never executives — their actual titles were as murky as their actual jobs. But guessing what they were used for was all too easy.

And then he was gone, pushing his way back through the crowd.

I did the same thing with my crowd. From what I could see, the quickest way to the other side was to run to the parking lot in back. I didn't get far. As I rounded the corner of the hotel a uniform appeared and held up his hand. He also raised his flashlight and burned the beam into my face.

"Hold on. You have some ID?"

"Look, Officer, there's somebody I need to see on the other side."

"You a guest in the hotel?"

"Yes."

He snapped his fingers and held his palm out, a thickset middle-aged man with dark, suspicious eyes and the mannerisms of a hall monitor.

The best thing to do was get it over as quickly as possible. When I handed him my wallet, the beam fell from my face to my ID. "From Chicago?"

"Yes. Look, I really am in a hurry."

"Who is it you need to see so bad?"

"Old college friend. Just spotted him in the crowd on the far side."

"You know a woman was killed here tonight."

"I know. But I didn't do it and neither did Paul."

"Paul?"

"My college friend." I was tempted to say that I was working with Susan Cooper but decided against it. I wanted to keep her name out of it. I could see over his shoulder. Cars were leaving, flashes of headlights turning the cop into silhouette.

He still had my wallet. "Dev Conrad."

"That's right."

He beamed his light on my driver's license again. He was either memorizing it or trying to levitate it. He frowned and handed it back. He'd been hoping to plant my ass on death row, but he hadn't been able to come up with a good enough reason. "Get out of here."

"Thanks."

He waved me past as a couple came up behind me. I walked when I wanted to run but running would only make me interesting to him again. The rear of the hotel was lined with Dumpsters. A loading dock protruded from the center of the building. Parking space was limited to fifteen yards of macadam.

The two cars closest to me were empty. The silver Pontiac near the alley had a driver. The red-headed man. His headlights came on and he started backing out.

I yelled for him to stop and darted toward him. He laid down a long strip of rubber getting the car into the alley. For three or four seconds I had a good look at him. The brutal appearance was lessened by his cold smile. He was under the impression this was some kind of game. Then he was gone in a fishtailing, tire-screaming exit that went on all the long way to the end of the alley. I couldn't even get close enough to identify the license plate.

When I turned back to the hotel, my good friend the cop was standing there. He looked happy. "Guess Paul didn't want to see you, huh?"

"Yeah. Guess not."

"How about letting me see that wallet again?"

"Why?"

"Why? Because I said so is why." He shook his head and addressed an unseen person. "He asks why."

I gave him my wallet. He flipped it open, then used the communicator on his shoulder. "Tell Detective Kapoor there's somebody here she should probably talk to."

"What the hell're you doing?"

He held up a finger to quiet me. "Right. I'll bring him to the back door now."

After he finished talking, I said, "This is a waste of time."

"Maybe to you, but this whole little deal is strange."

"What 'whole little deal'?"

"You're in a big hurry to get back here, and then this supposed friend of yours races away. Somebody was killed here tonight, and that makes this whole little deal suspicious. At least to me." He returned my wallet. "I'm covering my ass, man. You go in and talk to the detective and she asks you a few questions and you're out of here." Then: "This isn't Chicago. People're used to murders there. We aren't. Anybody look a little weird at all, they got to be questioned. Hell, I should've sent you to the detective when you came running around the corner."

No point in arguing. He was just doing his job, and by admitting that he was covering his ass he dropped the tough-guy stuff and became a human being. Still and all, I doubted if I'd invite him to my next birthday party.

The back door was under a long narrow canopy. He had to knock twice. While we were waiting, he said, "My name's Bob Sullivan, by the way." He was amused again. "In case you want to file any complaints. Badge number 205." He was a tough guy again.

Another uniform answered the door and led us through the kitchen and then the dining room and then out to the lobby. This late, everything had been shut down for a few hours anyway.

Three detectives had divided up the lobby. Each had a short line of people to interview. Most of the interviewees were hotel employees, but there was a handful of guests, too. Sullivan steered me to the shortest line. I assumed the detective I would be seeing was the slim woman in the dark-blue suit. She was talking to a bellhop. She was attractive in a dark silken way. Indian, I guessed.

"You want some coffee? They've got a big pot of it going over there." Sullivan nodded to a table that had been set up with snacks and coffee.

"Thanks."

Despite the line being short, I was on my

second cup of coffee by the time the detective was ready for me. She indicated a chair that had been brought in from the dining room. I sat down. There was a matching chair for her, but I'd yet to see her sit down. She offered me a long, slim hand and another smile. "I'm sure you want to get to your room as soon as possible, Mr. Conrad, so I'll make this as quick as I can."

"I'd appreciate that."

"My name is Detective Priya Kapoor. I'll bet you've never heard of a cop with that name before." Unaccented English. "I was born and raised in Chicago. I'm a White Sox fan."

I wondered how many hundreds of times she'd said this in her time on the force. "No, I never have." She wasn't beautiful but she was erotic, the dark velvet eyes and the wide tender mouth inspiring flare-ups of lust in my drained body. It had been a while.

"First of all, Mr. Conrad, I take it you're in town on business."

"Yes."

"Would you mind telling me what that business is?"

"I work with Congresswoman Cooper on her campaign." Usually an occupation wouldn't tell her anything. But Monica Davies had been in politics and so was I.

"I'm a political consultant."

"That's very nice. I voted for her." The cruise director voice again. I'm just a friendly lady going through the motions, Mr. Conrad, said the voice. But the erotic eyes had become the dubious eyes. "That's very interesting."

"Oh? How so?"

She sat down on the dining-room chair opposite me. The first time I'd seen her park her fine small bottom anywhere. "Mr. Conrad, it's late, as I said. So let me ask you, do you really want to put me — and yourself — through the charade of pretending that you didn't know Monica Davies?"

"I met her a few times, yes."

"Thank you. I appreciate that. You've saved both of us at least ten minutes. May I ask where you were tonight?"

"If you're asking for an alibi, I have a good one."

"Fine. Good alibis make my job a lot easier. Believe it or not, I enjoy eliminating people as persons of interest. That way I can concentrate on the guilty party."

"There was a fund-raiser for Congresswoman Cooper at the Royale Hotel tonight. I was there all evening. I didn't leave until about thirty or forty minutes ago."

"And I'm hoping that a good number of

people saw you."

"A large number of people. And all night long."

Somewhere in the pocket of her jacket her cell phone rang. "Excuse me."

I tried to make sense of her and the phone conversation, but I couldn't. The county morgue was mentioned. The rest of it was lost on me.

After putting her phone away again, she said, "Do you know Greg Larson, Ms. Davies's partner?"

"Yes."

"What do you think of him?"

"I'd rather not say."

"Why not?"

"Because we hate each other. Anything I'd say about him would be prejudiced."

"Why do you hate him?"

"It doesn't matter."

"It matters to me, Mr. Conrad."

My fingers started drumming on the table. As if I didn't control them.

"Mr. Conrad?"

"I'm in a business that can get dirty. I've been dirty myself and I'll be dirty again. But it's a matter of degrees. Most people on either side have lines they won't cross. Larson crosses them all the time."

"You're quite angry, Mr. Conrad. I can

see it on your face."

"You asked how I felt about Larson. I told you."

"Have you seen Mr. Larson?"

"Yes. He came to the fund-raiser tonight."

"Isn't that strange? Him coming to a fund-raiser for his opponent?"

I made it a joke. "He came to torment me."

"And did he succeed?"

"He sure did. I don't like being in the same room with him."

"Did you feel the same way about Monica Davies?"

"Pretty much. They both did the same kind of work."

"One more question, Mr. Conrad. The patrolman told me that you had some kind of altercation with somebody in a car behind the hotel a few minutes ago."

"It wasn't an altercation. I just wanted to say hello to an old friend."

"Apparently he didn't want to say hello to you. The officer told me that you were shouting at him and chasing after his car."

"He obviously didn't recognize who I was. He might not even have heard me. In college he always played the radio very loud."

Her sly smile was a review of my story. It closed opening night. "I'd never take up fiction if I were you, Mr. Conrad."

She stood up. "I see I have two more people I need to talk to, and I'm sure you're ready for some sleep." She offered her long, sleek hand. As I stood up I took it. She was strong. "I'm sorry I had to trouble you with all this."

"Doing your job."

She gave me her best broadest, emptiest smile. "Now, that's not what you're *really* thinking, is it?"

"No," I said as I started to turn away. "No, I guess it's not." I was too tired for any more of her droll inquisition.

"Give the female patrol officer all your contact information, if you would. I hope you have a good night's sleep."

I muttered through room number, phone number, home address, home telephone number, and headquarters phone number with the officer taking down all the information. Then I turned, yawning, toward the elevator.

■ ■ ■ ■

PART TWO

■ ■ ■ ■

CHAPTER 11

I got into headquarters just after seven the next morning. I'd spent forty-five minutes on the StairMaster in the hotel gym, then had an egg and a piece of toast and three cups of coffee in the café. I was the only one in the office for a time. I didn't want to think about Monica Davies and why Bobby had had her card and how Susan Cooper might be involved in all this. I forced myself to go through the internals that had been faxed late last night.

The difference between public polling and internal polling is sometimes complicated but generally comes down to the fact that internal polling is done in more depth. Public polling is about the horse race; internal polling goes after demographics — age, occupation, general political beliefs — and delves into issue details. Another factor is where respondents come from. Public polling tends to use random numbers from the phone books. Internal polling uses registered voters. What made me happy this morning was the sudden shift we were seeing in rural voters supporting Susan. We'd been lagging behind. But now we'd jumped up by four percent and that was encouraging. Same with blue-collar males. Duffy was still ahead with this group, but in the past week we'd added three percent blue-collar males. The trend was up, and we were sitting on a story tying Duffy to some union-busting operations done by two companies he owned part of. We had decided to hold these until the next debate. This would help us get more blue-collar votes.

Ben came in with his hand wrapped around a large paper cup of coffee and the scent of autumn morning on his clothes. "You don't look too bad."

"Thanks, neither do you."

"You think we're getting respectable in our old age?"

I laughed. "You're going to have us buried before our time."

He sat down at his desk. "Well, since you're so young and studly, did *you* get lucky last night?"

"Nope." Then I looked up from the internals I was still going over. The way he'd said it — "You mean *you* got lucky last night?"

He swiveled in his chair so I could see him and his big happy face. "Hold your applause, but yep, I did indeed get lucky last night. This reporter from Channel 6. The NBC affiliate. Forty-three and worried about her job with all these hotties coming right out of college and working for half of what she's making. I like her."

"Good. Now that you've lost your virginity I'll have to see about losing mine."

He pointed to the desk two down from his. "You know who sits there?"

"Oh, no. No, thanks."

"Last night Kristin told me that she had a very serious crush on you."

"She's too young."

"She's not that much younger."

"You know what happened last time."

"Hey, Kristin isn't like — what the hell was her name?"

"Donna."

"Kristin isn't like Donna. Donna was all fucked up." Pause. "Plus she was making it with Neil Ransom on the side, anyway. You know, when she was seeing you."

"Are you serious?"

"Yeah. That's why everybody in the office hated her. She was doing this stalking number on you, but she was also getting it on with Ransom."

"I thought they hated her because she was bragging about sleeping with the boss."

"Well, I'll be damned. You mean you really didn't know?"

Ben's phone rang. Just before he picked up, he said, "Well, I told Kristin I'd tell you that she'd like to go to dinner tonight. She ended up going out with her cousin last night and having a pizza." Then: "Hello?" And: "Who's calling, please?" He covered the speaking end of the receiver with his hand and said, "She sounds very young and very upset. Line three."

"No dinner, Ben. Seriously." I picked up my phone.

"Mr. Conrad?"

I recognized the voice immediately even through her tears. "Gwen?"

"You said I could call you."

"Yes. Of course. Are you all right?"

"I am, but Bobby isn't. He's in jail. They arrested him this morning. They said he killed that woman. Somebody saw him running from her hotel room. I'm scared for him and I'm scared for my baby."

Full circle. The motel room to the red-haired man to Monica Davies to Bobby. "Where are you now?"

"I'm at the police station. They won't let me see him."

"You stay there. I'll be right down."

"I'd really appreciate it, Mr. Conrad." Starting to cry. "He didn't kill her. He really didn't."

After hanging up, I said to Ben, "I need the name of a good criminal attorney in this town. Fast."

"What the hell's going on?"

"Just the name, Ben. I'll have to explain later."

"Well, one of our backers is a man named James Shapiro. Very good reputation. Very nice guy."

"Fine. Thanks. You got his number?"

A minute later I was talking to James Shapiro's secretary. "He's not in right now."

"I'm with the Cooper campaign. Dev Conrad. Something's come up and I really need to talk with him. I hate to lean on you this way, but it's important."

"Well, he's probably in court."

"Can you reach him there?"

"Yes, one of his people can get a message to him."

"Here's my cell phone number. I'll be in my car soon, but please have him call me as soon as possible."

"All right. Mr. . . . Conrad?"

"Yes. Conrad. Thank you."

I got directions to the police station from Ben.

"You got me scared, Dev. Young woman crying and a criminal defense lawyer . . ."

"It'd take too long to explain. And it's between you and me, obviously."

"Really? Shit, I thought I'd call the *Chronicle* and give them an exclusive."

Traffic was light so I moved quickly. I was getting close to the street I wanted when my cell phone toned.

"Mr. Conrad?"

"Thanks for calling, Mr. Shapiro."

"Jim. Please. You probably don't remember this, but we met one time at the governor's inauguration ball. Debby said it was an emergency. I just stepped out into the hall to call you. One of my associates is conducting the cross, anyway."

I told him what I knew without mentioning Susan. Just that I liked this young woman and wanted to help her.

"So you don't know anything about this Bobby?"

"Afraid I don't."

"Monica Davies, huh? I wish I could say she didn't have it coming."

"I feel the same way."

"All right, Dev, I'll be there. I need a little time, but I'll be there."

I pulled into the parking lot of the long, low, lean police station. The tan limestone exterior and the wide windows in front gave it an open feeling you don't find in many law enforcement facilities. I swung the car into an empty parking spot. "I'm at the police station now."

"I'm about six blocks from you. I need fifteen minutes, give or take. I'll see you then."

The same architectural feeling continued inside the police department. The walls were painted a light blue, the tile floors were a complementary darker blue, the lobby furnishings were modern but comfortable, and the front counter was held down by two attractive women in regular blouses and skirts, no uniforms of any kind. This might have been the office of a medical clinic. The grit was found in the back half of the building, the one where the windows were barred up and down.

I went to the counter and asked if Detective Priya Kapoor was here and if I could speak to her. One of the women told me to have a seat and she'd see if the detective was available. Then I asked her about Gwen. She said, all maternal rather than all cop, "She's in the bathroom being sick."

I sat down and started to wait. I'd been

there only a few minutes when the front doors opened and a sobbing woman and an angry man disrupted the busy but tranquil air.

The woman, mid-forties I guessed, worn from work and dashed dreams, sat in the seat across from me. She kept dabbing her face with her gnarled handkerchief and looking at me with watery blue despairing eyes. If she even saw me. Sitting there in her rumpled, fake leather jacket and blue jeans, she seemed to see beyond me, to some other terrible realm that was summoning her.

The man, now at the counter, had taken to shouting. "He took it for a little ride and brought it back! This is total bullshit! I want to see Cummings! That bastard has it in for my kid and won't give him a break!"

The woman didn't turn her head to watch her husband. But each time his voice got especially loud her body would jerk as if she'd been stabbed.

The man came over and sat down in the chair next to hers. He took her hand, a surprising bit of gentleness given his flinty face with its broken nose and scars across the left side of his throat, the same tender way Bobby treated Gwen. This man had a full dark gray-streaked beard and massive arms sticking out of his yellow sports shirt. His Bears cap had a union button on it.

She put her head to his shoulder and said, "This time they'll send him to a real prison, Bob. A real prison."

"Those sons of bitches," he said.

After my years in army intelligence, when I'd functioned pretty much as a detective, I'd thought about joining a police force somewhere. I'd spent three nights in a squad car riding around Chicago. The dangers I'd seen were tolerable; there'd been moments when they'd been exhilarating. But the heartbreak was what I couldn't handle. The beaten wives and the forlorn children, the sad junkies, the prisons of poverty, the people afraid to walk the streets of their own neighborhoods. I didn't have the gut for it.

I studied their faces as they slumped together across from me, the eternal grief of parents whose child is in serious trouble.

Detective Kapoor wore a wine-red blouse and a black skirt today. She was a dream of radiance and charm. "Mr. Conrad, if you'd like to follow me." She made no eye contact with the couple on the chairs.

"I'm meeting a lawyer here in a few minutes. A Mr. Shapiro."

The smile was enigmatic. "Oh, yes, Mr.

Shapiro."

I couldn't tell if her tone was disapproval or some kind of amusement. When I got to my feet I felt guilty a moment for deserting the couple across from me. As if I should have stayed with them in silent commiseration. But I was relieved, too. I had a desperate situation of my own to tend to.

Her office was small but organized with ruthless efficiency. God forbid that anything was out of place. She had a Mac and a window and a framed photograph of her with a very young girl who resembled her a good deal. Her desk was cleared and her pencils, six yellow ones, were lined up like bullets next to a small notepad.

"I'm wondering why you're here, Mr. Conrad. And what your interest is in Bobby Flaherty."

"I'm a friend of Mr. Flaherty's wife."

"I see. But a young woman like that — would you mind telling me how you know her?"

"I'm just a friend."

"So you've known her for a long time?"

"Not a long time. But some time."

This was her morning for enigmatic smiles. "Jim Shapiro doesn't come cheap."

"I assumed that was the case."

"And Mr. Flaherty certainly won't be able

to afford him."

"I assumed that would be the case, too."

"Will you be paying Mr. Shapiro's fees?"

"I haven't had a chance to talk about money with him yet. But I'm sure we'll work things out."

"I'm just surprised that you're so interested in this case."

"As I said, Gwen is a friend of mine."

The knock on the half-open door was perfunctory. A tall, trim, gray-haired man came into the office. He roiled the air with his sense of energy and purpose. He looked like one of those adventurous men you see in print ads for expensive brands of whiskey, the kind of masculine self-confidence juries love and prosecutors fear.

He carried a slender briefcase and a ready smile. "Watch out for her, Conrad. Her bite is much worse than her bark. I'm Jim Shapiro."

We shook hands and he took the empty chair next to me. "How's the beautiful Priya today?"

This time the smile wasn't enigmatic at all. She obviously liked Shapiro. "The beautiful Priya, as you say, is sitting here trying to figure out why Mr. Conrad is so interested in helping Mr. Flaherty."

"It's just his nature. Mr. Conrad's. Helping other people."

"You two have never met before now, have you?"

"Not technically, Priya. But how did you know that?"

"Body language. I make a study of it. You're two strangers sitting side by side. Which makes me all the more curious." She addressed her question to me. "Did you get Jim's phone number from the Yellow Pages?"

"Men's room wall," Shapiro said. "You know, 'For a good time call . . .' "They both laughed at his joke. Then: "Look, Mr. Conrad and I really do need to talk. How about you drifting off somewhere for about ten minutes and letting us use your office?"

She pushed back from her desk and said, "Actually, there is something I need to check on. But I can't give you more than ten minutes."

"Perfect. I really appreciate this."

As she came out from around her desk, the stylish cut of her skirt emphasizing the pleasing line of her long legs, she said, "Maybe in ten minutes you and Mr. Conrad can come up with a reasonable explanation for why Mr. Conrad is so interested in this case."

She left us with another one of her unreadable smiles. She was careful to close the door tight.

Shapiro jumped up and parked himself on the edge of her desk. "We can talk here. I've used this room before. Priya assured me it's not bugged."

"And you trust her?"

"We used to date for a while. We both got divorces at the same time. But you know how those kinds of relationships go. We weren't over our spouses. But anyway, she's a cool lady. And yes, I trust her." He rubbed his hands together as if savoring a hearty meal. "So what's this got to do with Susan?"

He knew how to cut through the bullshit. "What makes you think she's involved?"

"Dev, look, if we're going to work together, remember one thing — I've been around the block more than a few times. Okay? You arrive in town yesterday, Monica Davies is murdered, and here you are getting a lawyer for this Flaherty kid. Have you even met him?"

"Once."

"When and where?"

I described the motel scene. I didn't mention Susan's involvement.

"So you just happened to be cruising past this motel and you decided to pull in. And you just happened to find a room where this girl, Gwen, was crying. Two big coincidences there. Now, tell me how Susan plays into this."

"Attorney-client privilege?"

"Just give me ten bucks."

"In movies they only give the lawyer a dollar."

His grin took ten years away from his face. "Fuck movies. This is real life. Movies never get anything right anyway." Then he was serious again: "Now, where does Susan come into this?"

I told him what I knew, including the part about a witness seeing Bobby run away from Monica's hotel room. Shapiro had a small notebook tucked into his back pocket. He dug it out and started scribbling with one of Priya's carefully laid-out pencils.

"Wow," he said when I finished. "None of this makes any sense yet, does it?"

"Not to me. Susan obviously knows the Flahertys somehow."

"And yesterday morning she told you that everything is all right now?"

"That's what she said. But I've learned that she can suck it up and play it real happy even when it's all going to hell. That's what makes her such a good candidate."

"I want to talk to Gwen. See what she'll tell me."

The knock came. I yanked out my wallet. He saw a one peeking up and plucked it free. "This'll do." The grin again.

Detective Kapoor came back in and said, "I can take you back to where Mr. Flaherty is, if you'd like, Jim. And you don't have to worry about him having said anything damaging. He won't say anything at all."

She stood aside while I walked out into the hallway. When Shapiro walked out I said, "You have my cell phone number. Call me right away when you're finished."

The detective's dark eyes gleamed with amused suspicion. "Oh, yes, Mr. Conrad here is very interested in this case even though he can't explain why exactly."

Shapiro patted me on the back. "A good Samaritan if I've ever seen one."

Her eyes rested on me briefly. Then she turned back to the lawyer and they began walking to the far end of the hall. I walked to the lobby, hoping that Gwen was back.

The married couple was gone. Gwen, appearing to be younger and frailer than ever, sat with her hands clutched tight together staring at the opposite wall. Today she wore a faded brown maternity top that looked as if she'd bought it used. She didn't quit staring at the wall even when I sat down next to her. Her nose and eyes were a furious red. I took one of her hands and placed it in mine.

"I noticed a coffee shop about half a block from here. Why don't I buy you something to eat?"

"I'd just throw it up." Despite her appearance, her voice was strong, steady. "But I could use some tea."

I hoped the autumn day soothed her as we walked. The temperature was in the high fifties and the sun made the painted colors of the trees bright as copper. She eased along with her burden: young, sweet, lost. More than once I'd wondered if my interest in her was a form of repentance for being such an absent father to my own daughter while she was growing up. The siren call of elections had kept me on the road, and not until the last few years with my daughter back East in college had I gotten to know her.

The coffee shop was small and of another era with its chrome-bottomed counter stools and its hand-painted pine booths. I noticed photos of the previous owners — faded black-and-white pictures of a deceptively simpler time.

When my Danish came I sawed off a third of it, placed the slice on a napkin, and pushed it over to her side of the booth.

"Give it a try."

"I don't know if I can hold it down."

"Up to you. It's there if you get the urge."

She sipped her tea. "This is what I need. It's just been — we weren't even awake when they came. The police, I mean. We were down to our last few dollars, so we were in this real dive of a motel. It was a lot worse than the one we were in yesterday even. Bobby registered under our real name. That's how they found us."

"Why did they come after Bobby?"

"The drawing they made."

"A police composite?"

"Yeah, I guess that's what they call it. It was only on TV for a short time. The night clerk at the motel recognized Bobby and called the police." Her shoulders slumped and she was bound up in her misery. "He won't tell me anything about it. No matter how hard I beg him. He just keeps saying that he'll explain it to me someday. I'm having such a hard time with my pregnancy, and I'm so sick all the time that I haven't really paid much attention."

"Why was he at Monica Davies's hotel room?"

She looked exasperated. "I already told you. He wouldn't tell me anything."

"Monica Davies had a partner. Does the

name Greg Larson mean anything to you?"

"Oh, yes. That's the man who got into it with Bobby yesterday. The bloody towel you found."

Circles within circles within circles. Larson and Bobby Flaherty.

"He really scared me. Bobby made me go for a walk when Larson came. When I got back I heard them fighting. I was afraid Bobby might be hurt, so I rushed into the room. They were wrestling. Larson looked over at me when I came in, and Bobby shoved him. Larson hit his head against the edge of the bathroom door. He started to faint, I think, but then he managed to stagger over to the desk. That was when he fell down against the chair. The back of his head bled on the desk. I was screaming for them to stop. Bobby was scared then, too. He ran into the bathroom and soaked a towel under the shower and brought it out to Larson. He made Larson sit down and see if he was all right. I could see Larson was real mad, but he was worried about his head, so he had to concentrate on that. Bobby even offered to drive him to the ER. That's why it's so crazy to say that Bobby killed anybody. He really freaked out when he saw that he'd hurt Larson."

I had to weigh her words here against the

words Bobby had been flinging at me as we fought yesterday. He had a temper for sure, but the way he took care of Larson made me wonder if he had any killer instinct. Or maybe he was just worried about his own fate. It's easy to be naive about criminality.

"Why was Larson there?"

"I don't know. Bobby wouldn't tell me."

"Had you ever seen him before?"

"Twice. He came at night and Bobby left with him. Bobby was pretty drunk when he got back, but he still wouldn't tell me anything." Her gaze had fallen on the piece of Danish I'd cut for her. "I guess I'm getting hungry."

"Why don't you eat that and I'll order you anything else you want."

"I don't like being a mooch."

"I'm treating you. That's not being a mooch."

Those deep green eyes watched me for a few seconds. "I can't pay you back."

"I don't expect you to."

"I don't mean just with money. I mean I can't even tell you anything about what's going on. Because I don't know myself."

"Maybe we'll find out together."

The moods were fast as light, shifting in texture and color. The lower lip trembled and the eyes filled. "Our poor baby. Not even born yet and his father is in jail. That's what I'm worried about."

The waitress was nearby. She came over when I waved at her. "Why don't you bring Gwen here her own Danish?"

"Sure." She finished writing on her ticket pad and said, "Be right back."

"I don't know if I can eat that."

"You'll be surprised. My ex-wife always said that, too. Then she'd clean out the refrigerator."

Gwen smiled and some of the sadness left her eyes and mouth. "Yeah, I was thinking it's sort of like those models do. They have that — what do you call it? — where they eat and then throw up?"

"Bulimia."

"Yeah. But even with that I've managed to put on a lot of weight."

I couldn't help it. I laughed. "You've put on weight? What did you weigh before? Ninety pounds?"

"No. I weighed a hundred and now I'm a hundred and ten. All the women in my family are small. Actually, so are the men; for men they're small, I mean."

The Danish came. She ate shamelessly while I sat and watched her. She wiped out the Danish in a few bites and then sat back, sated. "Boy, I guess I was hungrier than I thought." A sigh. "But I feel guilty. Bobby's in jail and here I am stuffing my face."

"I'm told Jim Shapiro is a very good defense attorney."

"Bobby didn't kill that woman."

"Did he ever mention her — Monica Davies?"

"No. Never."

"How long have you been in town here?"

"Ten days. I always count them."

"You've never told me what brought you here."

"I'm not sure. We've never had much money. Bobby told me that maybe he could get some kind of steady gig here. You know, with a band that played five or six nights a week. You can make pretty good money when you do that. I pretty much believed that when Bobby started talking about it. But the more I thought about it, the more I started thinking that maybe that was just an excuse. That maybe there was something else going on that Bobby didn't want me to know about. And then when Larson started coming around, I knew I was right. But I still didn't have any idea what was going on. That's one thing Bobby and I have always argued about — he just kind of sneaks off and does stuff and never explains himself. The funny thing is that I trust him

133

— you know, where other girls are concerned. I really don't think he cheats on me. But I wish he'd tell me where he goes when he takes off like that." Talking that much seemed to have tired her. She placed her hands reverently over her belly and closed her eyes briefly. "I'm just so worried about him."

I wanted to ask her about Susan Cooper again. But right now she didn't need any more grief.

"Why don't we head back to the police station and find out what's going on?"

She sat up straight, eyes open, and said, "God, I don't know what I'd do if you hadn't come along." Then she started her awkward slide out of the booth. I was thinking how good it would be when my own daughter was pregnant. I had so much to make up for. I wanted to do it right this time.

We sat in the lobby for half an hour before Jim Shapiro appeared. Gwen made two trips to the bathroom. She got thirsty and I managed to find a 7UP for her. On cue, five minutes after drinking the pop, she went to the bathroom again.

Shapiro appeared in a rush. He didn't look happy. He took us to a corner in a kind of huddle. He put his hand on Gwen's shoulder and said, "Honey, I've arranged for you to see your husband for fifteen minutes. I need you to do me a favor." He glanced at me before he finished. "I need you to make him understand that this is a very serious charge and that I can't help him if he won't help me." He took his hand from her shoulder. He frowned in my direction. "He said he doesn't know Larson and that he never met Monica Davies." Back to her: "He's lying. He also says that he doesn't know Congresswoman Cooper, but if that's true why did Dev here see her go into your motel room yesterday? Do you see what I mean?"

"Yes." She touched her stomach. I wondered if she was in pain.

"Tell him that for your sake and the sake of your child he has to tell me everything he knows about Larson and Monica and Congresswoman Cooper. They all tie together."

"Won't Congresswoman Cooper tell you anything?" Then she frowned at me. "I should've told you I knew her, Mr. Conrad."

"That's all right."

He looked at me again. "I'll be talking to Dev about that while you're in seeing Bobby. Now, you see that officer over there by the desk?" She nodded. "He's waiting for you. He'll take you back to see your husband."

"I'm scared, Dev."

"You'll do fine."

She walked over to the officer waiting for her.

"Listen, Dev, I'm due in court in half an hour, and I need to swing by my office before I go there. I'm not getting anywhere with Bobby right now, so that means you have to get somewhere with Susan. I don't know what the hell's going on here, but she's involved somehow and that's going to lose her the election. I'll do this pro bono — tell her that — because that's how much I want her to win. But, man, I have to know what I'm dealing with." Then he caught himself and said: "They'll probably bring Gwen back here. But Priya will grab her if she sees her and start asking questions. I don't want that to happen before I get something from Bobby. Get Gwen out of here as fast as you can and hide her someplace."

I was back sitting in the lobby again. A pair of wannabe Hell's Angels came in sneering and giggling and giving the woman at the counter grief. They said they were waiting to see a Detective Walker. A female uniform walked by, and one biker nudged the other, then pointed to his groin and ground his hips. The other one laughed with teeth that would have done a caveman proud. Finally a male uniform the size of a beer truck and with the disposition of a crocodile came out and laid a manila folder on the reception desk. He had some business with the receptionist. She nodded to the bikers and rolled her eyes. They were making pistols of their fingers and aiming them at two detectives in a glassed-in office. The officer sidled over to them and said, "Why don't you boys go over there and sit down? Darla here'll call you when Walker's available." They gave him no problem whatsoever.

They walked over and sat down in chairs facing me. I was wearing a suit, which seemed to make them giddy. They did a lot of communicating with their elbows. A fun couple.

Gwen came slow and gray out into the open area in front of the reception desk. She didn't seem to quite know where she was. I was out of my chair immediately.

She leaned against me. I wondered if she was going to pass out. I got my arm around her shoulder and we started to leave the station. The bikers said something and giggled again. I'd have to stop back and kill them later. I'd be bringing an Uzi. I hurried her down the steps as soon as possible. I was waiting for Detective Kapoor to shout at our backs that she wanted to question Gwen.

There was a concrete bench half a block down. I helped her over there and we sat down. She put her head against me. I hugged her. I could smell her hot tears. There was nothing to say for now, so I just sat there holding her.

Cars and people came and went. Smoky melancholy autumn was on the breeze briefly and it was jack-o'-lantern time for a moment. I imagined Gwen dressing her little boy or girl up to go trick-or-treating. She'd have a good time taking the little one around all got up in costume with a bag ready for plunder. And all this misery would be forgotten. Or so I hoped.

She gathered herself in a self-conscious way. She stood up, drew her hands down her cheeks to dry her tears, then walked around in tight little circles taking deep breaths. People going into the station gawked at her, of course, but if she noticed she didn't seem to care.

Then she came back and sat down and said, "You need to talk to Susan Cooper. I wasn't supposed to mention her name, but right now I don't know what else to do. They usually send me out of the room when they talk. But I think I've pretty much figured out who she is."

"She's his mother."

"How did you guess? They don't look alike at all."

"She's taking a lot of risks. And hurting her campaign. She wouldn't do that unless she was really involved with Bobby in some way."

"One night Bobby was crying and she was holding him and rocking him back and forth like a little child. That was when I knew she was his mother. But he won't talk about her to me. And he won't talk about Craig, either."

"Who's Craig?"

"I'm not sure. But he scares me. And sometimes he gives Bobby money."

"What's he look like?"

"He has red hair for one thing. He's big, too. And he always — I don't know how to say it — it's like he's always ready to explode. That's why he's dangerous."

"Do you know his last name?"

"I only heard it once. Craig Donovan, I think."

"And Bobby won't talk to you about either of them?"

"He just says we're going to have some serious money pretty soon. That's how he always says it, 'serious money.' But when I ask him, he says I'm better off not knowing and that I'd just worry if I knew."

"C'mon," I said.

"Where're we going?"

"I'm going to find you a decent motel. I'm hoping Jim Shapiro can get Bobby out pretty soon."

"Really?"

"Jim's good. And if all they have on Bobby is that he was seen running from Monica's room, I doubt they can hold him much longer."

It was nice to see her smile.

CHAPTER 12

David Manning was climbing into his shiny, new silver Aston Martin convertible when I pulled into the headquarters parking lot. He wore tan slacks and a navy-blue blazer over an open-collared white dress shirt. He might have passed for dapper if his face wasn't so drawn and his glance so tired. When he saw me he reversed course and came out of his car.

"Morning, Dev."

"Morning, David."

"Just stopped by to see if my wife had turned up yet."

"She's not inside?"

"No. And nobody seems to know where she is, either."

The side door to the headquarters opened. Doris Kelly emerged and started walking toward us. Her pale blond hair caught the sun. In her shy way, she was a compelling woman, one of those quiet ones who become more interesting the longer you're around them.

"Sorry I kept you, David. I just wanted to call and see how they were treating my mother at the nursing home. She just moved in yesterday."

"That's fine, Doris. How's she doing?"

"Well, so far she likes it." The shy smile again. "Of course, it's just been twenty-four hours." She turned to me. "I guess they're having trouble finding Susan again."

"That's what David was saying. Was she home last night?"

"Got home late," David said. "I waited up for her till about two and then just went up to bed."

"You really need your sleep, David," Doris said. "You work so hard."

He laughed. "She not only helps me at the foundation; she's also my substitute mother." He touched a gentle hand to her shoulder. "Don't worry, Mom. I get plenty of sleep."

"But Susan did come home, David?" I asked.

"Yes. I'm not sure what time. But she was there when the maid served breakfast. She told me she was at Jane Clarke's after the fund-raiser."

"I guess I don't know that name."

"Her best friend for years. They were inseparable for a long time. They had a little falling-out. Now they're close again. She probably would have said more, but then Natalie came downstairs."

"It didn't go well?"

His mouth tightened. "Natalie started in on Susan about how she's been doing this wrong and that wrong. You know Natalie when she gets going. I tried to get her to back off a little. . . ." The way his voice trailed off indicated that he hadn't had much luck. But then I'd seen him with Natalie. He was her prisoner, but instead of a gun she wielded a checkbook.

Doris's blue eyes narrowed. "They're always putting you in the middle, David."

He smiled at me. "My defender here." He checked his watch. "We've got a meeting at the foundation in fifteen minutes. We need to get going. I'm sorry this campaign seems to be coming apart for you, Dev. But I think Susan will come around. She usually does."

The word that stayed in my mind was "usually."

Inside, Kristin and Ben were both on their phones. I sat down at a free computer and started checking my e-mail. I decided against sending money to a Nigerian prince who promised to swell my bank account into a fortune, against purchasing a "male enhancement" drug that would make me the envy of all the guys in the locker room and ensure that the ladies would be lined up around my block, and against signing a petition to investigate our current president to see if he was an extraterrestrial. After that I logged on to the Web site of the local newspaper and saw a photograph of Greg Larson. The headline read CONTROVERSIAL POLITICAL CONSULTANT QUESTIONED BY POLICE.

Now I was sure Bobby would be back on the street sometime today. If the police were talking to Larson, then something must have happened to make him seem suspicious to them. There had been rumors for a year that Larson and Monica no longer got along. The story on the Web site indicated that they were in Aldyne because a political magazine wanted to do a lengthy profile of them. And this was a congressional seat that their party definitely wanted to win. The piece said they'd been here for five days.

I didn't see who walked in the door because I was busy on the computer, but when I heard Kristin say, "Thank God," I knew it had to be Susan.

"Morning, everybody. I thought I'd get a

workout in before the day started. I'm ready to go to the luncheon, Kristin, if you are."

I logged off the computer. By now Susan was walking to the coffeemaker. She took it black. She wore the usual impeccable suit — this one in dark brown — and two-inch heels. She must have sensed me watching her, because when she turned around she had her smile prepared and it was a good one. You couldn't go wrong with that smile. It made me reconsider sending off for that male-enhancement deal.

"Morning, Dev. Everybody seemed to have a good time last night."

"Yeah," I said, "except Monica Davies."

She was way too good at covering herself to do anything dramatic. But it was there in her eyes, tiny pinpoints of panic when the name came up. Bobby Flaherty to Larson to Monica to Susan Cooper. And now another name, the red-haired man, Craig Donovan.

"Well, as much as I disliked her, I didn't want her to die, Dev. I'm not very good at playing God."

"Somebody sure as hell was," Ben said, heading for the coffee himself. "Crushed her skull."

"The police are questioning Larson," Kristin said. She stayed at her desk. "The

145

tabloids are going to go crazy."

"I wonder if they'll start looking into all the rumors about those two," Ben said. "You know, that Georgia congressman they worked for that time basically said they were blackmailing him. But then he shut up all of a sudden."

"He shut up because the party got to him," I said. "The same way we've gotten to a few of our boys sometimes. Nobody wants the kind of investigation that would lead to. The congressman got elected, his kid got a cushy lobbying job in Washington, and for dropping his charges they helped him set up one of those nonprofit foundations where a good ole boy can get rich if he's careful."

"Yeah," Ben said, "standard operating procedure in Washington."

"Including a lot of our own people."

Ben laughed. "You know, sometimes I swear you're a spy working for the other side."

"I just want to keep reminding myself that we're just about as dirty as they are."

"Just about. But not quite."

"We've sure had our moments, Ben."

He smiled. "Yeah, but we don't talk about them."

Kristin was putting on her coat. Her red

hair was more vivid than ever. She had a hard time not looking glamorous.

"We'll see you in a while," Susan said, still treating me to that bullshit smile. She had to be wondering how long she could elude me. I was starting to wonder the same thing.

When they were gone I asked Ben, "You ever meet a friend of Susan's named Jane Clarke?"

"Oh, yeah. Couple times. Very nice woman. Why?"

"I think I'll go see her."

"Susan said she took back her own name after she got divorced. She should be in the phone book." He picked up the local one and handed it to me. "I should tell you, I had a crush on her for about three hours one night when we all went out to get pizza."

"Three hours," I said. "That's a record for you, isn't it?"

Ben laughed. "Almost."

The area the Google map directed me to had the look of a movie set. The McMansions were set against a couple of miles of autumn trees, blazing with the ironic beauty of death. Behind them ran the river and on the far side of the water there were hills packed tight with more trees. The pretentiousness of the houses intruded on the natural splendor. The streets and the false fronts could deceive the movie cameras but not the closer scrutiny of a passerby. I had the same feeling here, the stagey boastful way these homes presented themselves suggesting an emptiness inside.

Jane Clarke's house was either a Spanish-themed Tudor or a Tudor-themed Spanish hacienda. Both styles fought for dominance. The long rolling lawn was mostly topsoil, and the few trees looked as if they wouldn't be mature even by the end-time, when God or George W. Bush came back to take care of us once and for all. I thought of a story about some rich Southerner who'd built a huge McMansion that closely resembled the White House. It even had an oval office. I assumed Jane Clarke's house would have at least six bathrooms, with plasma TVs in at least two of them.

The doorbell resonated throughout the house. It was a full minute before I heard footsteps, tiny ones, working their way to the door. I wasn't sure why she looked familiar, but she did. She was attractive, dark-haired, and shiny with sweat. She was Susan's age, no doubt, early forties. Her white T-shirt and red shorts looked damp. They also were filled out so well, I'd doubtless be thinking of her throughout the day.

"Oh, great. A good-looking guy finally comes here and I'm all sweaty from the stationary bike." She had a nice big inviting smile. "Hi, Dev. I saw you at the fund-raiser. Susan pointed you out."

"That's right. That's why you look familiar. I saw you with her."

She opened the door wider. "I've got coffee on in the kitchen. Go pour yourself a cup. I'll take a quick shower and then we can talk." As I stepped into the vestibule, she said, "You're worried about Susan and I'm worried about Susan. But I won't tell you anything that will hurt her."

The kitchen was big enough for a small restaurant: hardwood flooring like the entire downstairs, two refrigerators, a butcher-block table that could have accommodated a cow, two sinks, two stoves, and an espresso machine. There was a built-in coffeemaker for those pedestrian thinkers who didn't want espresso and the inevitable wine storage units. I got myself some coffee and sat in one of the chairs by the huge window that overlooked the russet-and-gold hills behind the house. Spread across the table in front of me were pages of houses that some Realtor had provided. The houses were the kind I liked, old-fashioned with porches and venerable trees and sidewalks, homes likely built in the boom after the big war.

She burst into the kitchen saying, "Sorry I took so long."

"I watched the clock. Less than ten minutes."

"That's why my hair's still wet."

I watched the way her backside moved when she poured coffee. She had a sweet little bottom and short but graceful legs. I liked her a ridiculous amount.

When she sat down across from me, she said, "Is it all right if I take this towel off my head?"

"Sure."

She patted the towel on her hair one last time and then swept it away. In the light now I could see the wrinkles around her mouth and hazel eyes and the tiny point where her nose had probably been broken a long time ago. But to me she was all the more appealing for the wrinkles. I was at the age when I wanted women who were at least as road-tested as I was. She took a sip from her coffee and sat back and smiled. She'd changed into a pink top and jeans, and somehow the pink made her smile even more fetching.

"Couple things first," she said. "I hate this house, in case you're wondering. This was my husband's idea. He was in a dick-measuring contest with all the other lawyers in his firm. He left me because my warranty had expired. He met a lady lawyer at a convention in Chicago. She's beautiful, so I can't blame him there. But, of course, I *do* blame him. I used to hope there was a little gallantry left in this world, but my husband proved there wasn't. He handled the whole thing very badly. But I got a decent settlement and I got this house. I'm trying to sell this place so I can move into a house like the one I grew up in. My father was a high-school history teacher. We weren't used to luxuries."

"I was looking at some of these sheets. Looks like you wouldn't have much trouble finding the kind of place you want."

"The problem is the economy. This is an expensive house. And a lot of lawyers are being laid off in most of the big firms. Even a few of the CEOs Sean knew — Sean was my husband — they don't have the kind of money they once had, either."

"That doesn't exactly break my heart."

"From what Susan has told me about you, I didn't think it would. She told me you were a commie. And a very cynical man. But that she trusted your judgment and liked you very much."

"The only part of that I don't agree with is the commie part. They aren't radical enough."

"You and my soon-to-be ex would get along fine. He thinks everybody in your party should be put in prison."

"He sounds like a lot of fun."

"He was for a long time. But you know how marriages go."

"All too well. But I suppose Susan told you about that, too."

"She said that two of your staffers told her that you seemed lonely to them."

"That would be Ben and Kristin. And they both seem lonely to me, so I guess we're even."

"How about some more coffee?"

"Fine. But I can get it."

When I started filling my cup she said, "I like a man who knows his way around the kitchen. You know how to pour your own coffee."

Coming back to the table I said, "I have the home video. I studied it very hard for a week. I made a lot of mistakes — I kept pouring it on the floor — but I finally figured it out."

"Smart-ass. What I meant was my soon-to-be ex assumed that since I didn't have a job as such — not that he *wanted* me to

have a job, by the way — I should beco
his personal servant. Whatever he wanted
did. Susan saw the bind I was in a long ti:
before I realized it myself."

"And speaking of Susan."

She sighed and shrugged slender shoi
ders. "You want to find out what's upse
ting her so much, but there are some thin
I won't discuss. She's been my best frier
since seventh grade, when my family move
here. Even when she went away to privat
school we stayed in very close touch. Th
only time we didn't get along was when sh
got into drugs and sleeping around. I did
little bit of both myself, but I pulled back
while there was still something left of me.
Susan seemed determined to destroy herself. I couldn't handle watching it."

I meant to startle her, and I did. "And
somewhere during that time she had a son.
His name's Bobby Flaherty and he's in
town now."

She'd been reaching for her coffee bu
withdrew her hand. "I can't believe she tol
you that. She swore me to absolute secrecy.

"I figured it out for myself. She's bee
avoiding me so that we won't have t
discuss it."

"How did you 'figure it out'?"

"A couple of things happened and

seemed like the only explanation. But I need you to give me your impression of her the past few weeks. She's been missing scheduled campaign stops and she really blew off the last debate with Duffy. As a cynical commie, I'm worried about the campaign."

"But you're not worried about Susan?"

"I like Susan and I admire Susan, but I wasn't hired to be her shrink. I was hired to get her elected. So that's my main concern right now. And this thing with Bobby has obviously taken its toll on her."

She was up and crossing the hardwood floor to the coffeepot before she said, "She loves him very much."

"I assumed she did."

When she came back she said, "There's only one thing I'll tell you."

"All right."

"And I'll only tell you this because the two times I've asked her about it she just dismisses it, tells me I'm imagining things." She picked up her cup and blew on the coffee. "There's a man who followed us a few times. A redheaded man. She said she's never noticed him and therefore I'm crazy. But one night after we had dinner downtown I dropped her off at campaign headquarters. Her car was there. We said good night and I drove off. But when I got to the

end of the alley I looked in my rearview mirror, and I saw him pull in right next to her. And she walked over to his car. I went around the block and got as close as I could to them without being seen. They were standing there talking. They both looked very angry. I went around again, but this time their cars were gone."

"Did you tell her about what you saw?"

"I tried to last night, but she was so depressed about everything I didn't want to push it."

"So she spent most of the night here?"

"Yeah, it was like being in college again. We sat up all night and talked. It was nearly five o'clock when she left."

"You think she cares about the election?"

"Very much. She's really ambitious now. I sort of kidded her one night and said, 'You've had a taste of power and you want more.' And she said, 'It's terrible, Jane. But it's true.' "

I finished my coffee and said, "Well, thanks for the coffee and the company. I should have called before I came out here, but I figured you'd just stall me if I gave you a chance."

"I would have. But I'm glad you came."

She walked me to the front door. "Do you mind if I'm a little bit forward?"

"Be my guest."

"If you don't have any plans for tonight, would you consider having dinner with me somewhere?"

"You beat me to it. I was just about to ask you the same thing."

"Dammit. So much for staying cool and mysterious. I blew my chance."

"I'll call you later when I find out a little more about how the day is going to go."

I walked out into the smoky scent of autumn. The sky was as pure blue as a baby's eyes. As I was opening my car door I glanced back at the house. She was in the open doorway waving to me. It felt so damned good I forgot completely about being a cynical commie.

CHAPTER 13

The call came when I was only a few blocks away from campaign headquarters. The plan was to use the McDonald's drive-through and eat in the office. The call offered me a new and unwelcome alternative.

"How did you get this number?"

"My name's on your screen, huh?"

"What the hell do you want?"

"I got the number from Ben. I convinced him it was important. I want us to have lunch together. Since we're staying in the same hotel, that shouldn't be any big hassle."

"The answer is no and I'm going to end this conversation."

In a singsong voice he said, "I know something about Susan that you don't know."

"I doubt that."

"She's in trouble and you know it. And

I'm serious about knowing something you don't."

Nobody ever accused Greg Larson of not being clever. There was no way I could hang up now. "We can talk about it right now. I don't need to have lunch with you."

"Then you're a fool, Dev. This is serious shit."

I saw the McDonald's a block ahead. I didn't want to give him the pleasure of telling him that I'd meet him.

He did it for me. "Fifteen minutes in the Governor's Room. You know where it is."

He clicked off.

Ten minutes later I was angling my rental up into the parking garage that was attached to the hotel. From there I found an elevator that took me to the ground floor. Larson was sitting in a wing chair reading *The Wall Street Journal.* When he saw me, he folded the paper and stood up. He was a heavy man who somehow retained his good looks despite the whiskey flush on his face and the bulge above his belt line. Expensive and clever tailoring helped, as did the startling white hair. He had a boardroom gravitas that intimidated most people who didn't know any of the things he'd done. He started to put out his hand but then stopped. "I don't suppose you'd want to shake."

"Let's get our food and you tell me what's so important. I don't want to be around you any longer than I have to."

"It's a good thing I'm not sensitive. Otherwise you'd have hurt my feelings with that remark." I knew actors who would beg for his teeth. They were bright beauties. "It's because of Bill Potter, isn't it?"

"I said let's go eat."

"He was a poor candidate."

"He was an honorable man. He lost both his legs in Iraq and he had a promising career in the Senate."

"His father was a leftist and his brother was a fag."

I took two steps toward him. I was happy to see the fear spoil his central-casting face. "Listen to me, you piece of shit. Don't push it or I'll take you apart right here. You understand me?"

I'd spoken louder than I'd intended. His eyes scanned the lobby to see if anybody was aware of what was going on. I turned and walked toward the Governor's Room, the main restaurant so named because a governor in the early part of the last century had come from Aldyne. His bearded scowl hung from every wall.

We took a table that overlooked the river. Fishermen lined the far shore. They were likely much happier than I was at the moment.

Larson ordered a double scotch and water. I ordered a cup of coffee.

"Think you'll get me drunk and I'll tell you everything?"

"Just tell me what you want to tell me."

"The ladies must really like your idea of foreplay."

He waited until the waitress had brought our drinks and taken our orders and then he said, "Monica and I were about to dissolve our partnership." He must have expected some dramatic response from me. I just stared at him. "I found out what she'd been up to the last three or four years." I still said nothing. "Are you interested in this or not?"

"Not so far. Why would I care if two sleaze-bags didn't want to work together anymore?"

He sat back, folded his hands on the table, and frowned. "I have to admit I probably went a little overboard on Potter. But it was a close race, Dev. I hit him with the only thing I could."

"His father's a decent man and so is his brother."

"I guess that's where we differ. If the old man is so 'decent,' why is he such a socialist?"

"Universal health care makes him a socialist?"

"Hell, yes, it does. And you know what I'm talking about. Some of the op-eds he wrote against going to war in Iraq bordered on treason."

"You'd better look up treason, Larson. You don't know what the word means. And all he said was that we were being lied to. That hardly qualifies as treason."

"And his brother — that state doesn't want some flaming faggot to be its senator's brother. Especially when he's always pushing for gay marriage and gay adoption."

I smiled. I couldn't help myself.

"What's so funny?"

"I'm sitting here talking to some fop with manicured fingers who's had two or three face-lifts and two turns at liposuction. You're the flamer, Larson. Not Dave Potter. He's like his brother Bill. He did two tours in Iraq when it was at its worst. So knock off the phony John Wayne bullshit. And Wayne was a draft dodger, in case you've forgotten."

"That was a nice little speech."

"Bill Potter was a good senator and a

decent man. Unlike the hack you got elected. I was surprised he didn't show up wearing his white sheet and carrying a torch."

"Very funny."

"So what the fuck do you want? I'm giving you three minutes to lay it out or you'll be eating both of our lunches by yourself."

Out came the salads, came a refill of coffee for me, came the fresh hot bread.

"I found out that Monica was blackmailing three of our clients. One of them was Natalie Cooper." He was pleased with himself. He'd gotten my attention. But my silence made him uneasy. He hurried on. "That's why somebody killed her."

"And you, of course, didn't know anything about the blackmail?"

"I'm ruthless. I'm not stupid. Monica was both. She went through our money as soon as we got it. She even tried to convince me we needed a private jet. But she was a good front for our firm. She was good on TV and the cable boys didn't hate her the way they hate me. So she was useful. But she was greedy and so she got into blackmail."

"If she didn't cut you in, how did you find out about it?"

"I had her computer hacked. She was smart enough to never say anything outright, but after I read a few hundred e-mails it became clear what she was doing."

"Why are you telling me? Shouldn't you be telling the police?"

"You're losing your savvy, Dev. The police know there was a lot of friction between Monica and me. A couple of people in the hotel told them about our shouting matches. They wouldn't mind pinning her death on me. The press would love it. It'd be like seeing Karl Rove in a perp walk. You people would be having multiple orgasms if you saw something like that. So I'm sure as hell not going to let them know that I had a good reason to *want* to kill her."

Our food came. I had no appetite. I stuck to coffee. He started sawing on his rare steak immediately. After his cheeks were puffed out with meat and his lips glistened with blood, he said, "And there's another reason. If any of this ever hits the press, I need you to verify that I told you all this. If I'd had anything to do with the blackmail, I sure as hell wouldn't have told you about it."

"Because if the story gets out about blackmail, you're out of business whether you had anything to do with it or not."

"You don't have to sound so goddamn happy."

I pushed my plate away and then pushed my chair back.

"Where the hell are you going?"

"I have work to do."

"I tell you all this and you just get up and leave without saying anything?"

"Looks that way, doesn't it?"

I threw down a ten for the tip and left the Governor's Room. The old fart in all the framed photographs and paintings looked crabbier than ever.

CHAPTER 14

The Cooper estate stretched across a sprawling piece of land that was partly forest and partly field inhabited by the massive stone Tudor-style great house and the lesser servants' quarters and the stables where the horses were kept. Senator Cooper had bred and raised trotters. The white fences were stark in the bright afternoon. I pulled up on the circular drive and parked in front of the place. I stood for a moment watching a man walking a horse in from the field to the stables. There was something timeless about it, like a French pastoral painting. The door had a leaded-window insert and was made of half-timber paneling. I had the feeling a tonsured monk might open it.

A friendly woman in a russet-colored dress greeted me. The white hair framed a handsome face that had likely persevered seventy-some years in this vale of tears. "Yes, may I help you, sir?"

"My name is Dev Conrad. I need to see Mrs. Cooper."

"Oh, yes, Mr. Conrad. Please come in. My name is Winnie Masters. I'm Mrs. Cooper's secretary."

My feet echoed on a gleaming dark floor as she led me through an entry hall that was probably as big as the tiny house where my ex-wife and I spent our first two years. This house felt like a museum, and I didn't like it at all. As we moved down a hall I began to notice an endless number of framed photographs on the walls. The late senator and Natalie in meet-and-greets with everybody from Bill Clinton to Nelson Mandela to Bono.

As we continued our trek I noticed a formal dining room to the left. There was enough room for a good share of the United Nations to eat there. Winnie Masters finally stopped when we reached another Tudor door. This one hadn't required three trees to build, but it still had the sturdy and somewhat forbidding air of all such doors. Winnie opened it, then stood aside while I walked into a timbered den filled with icons of many different eras. The enormous floor-to-ceiling bookcases contrasted with the largest plasma screen I'd ever seen. The snapping flames in the brick fireplace seemed out of place in a room where a dozen theater seats were set in front of a movie screen partially covered with a curtain. There was a dry bar in a far corner. Before she directed me to a deep leather chair, Winnie Masters produced a quaint little coffee cup and said, "Do you take anything in your coffee, Mr. Conrad?"

"No, thanks."

Cup and saucer in my hand, my weight sinking into the luxury of the leather chair, I sat back and gawked around.

"This was the senator's favorite room."

"I'll bet."

"The rolltop desk over there came from one of Jack Kennedy's homes. The senator worked in the White House when President Kennedy was in office. I don't think he ever got over what happened that day in Dallas. Mrs. Cooper has told me that he still had nightmares about it right up to the time of his own death. He was very proud that he was able to get that desk."

"I'm sure he was."

"I never knew Senator Cooper, of course; I only came here after he died to help sort through his papers. Then Mrs. Cooper asked me to stay on, and it's been quite interesting. After my own husband died, I thought my life was over. But working here

— well, as I say, it's quite interesting."

I wondered how much she knew about any of it. If you want to know the skinny on a hospital, ask a nurse; if you want to know the secrets of a corporation, ask the executive secretary; if you want to know anything about a sociopathic former starlet, do you talk to her factotum?

"Have you seen Susan today?"

I liked the way she handled it: "Now please, Mr. Conrad, you don't expect to get me in the middle of all this, do you?"

"I thought I'd give it a try." I liked her smile and I liked her.

"You know what a spear carrier is in theater?"

"Sure."

"That's what I am in this household. I deliver messages. I don't interpret them and I don't enhance them in any way. I like it here because it's interesting and because I have a very nice room on the third floor. I don't want to leave."

"So you can't be bribed?"

"Not unless you're willing to pay for all seven of my grandchildren's college educations." The blue eyes held intelligent amusement. "Now, why don't I go and see if Natalie's busy?"

I always look over the books in libraries,

private or public. There was one section that was essentially Americana. The novels ran to Sherwood Anderson, John Dos Passos, Ernest Hemingway, Willa Cather, F. Scott Fitzgerald — novelists he might have read when he was in college back in the fifties. There was also a good deal of nonfiction, notably books by Saul Alinsky, the Chicago man who taught poor people how to organize and challenge those who held them down. He was a true champion of the downtrodden. His life was threatened many times by those who claimed he was a communist, but he continued on anyway. His books inspired millions of young people. I took down a copy of *Reveille for Radicals* and turned back the cover.

For my favorite wild-eyed radical
From his loving wife Patricia

They'd been married twenty years before her heart finally gave out. From all I'd read about the couple Patricia was as progressive as her husband. She'd been a sociology student at Alinsky's alma mater, the University of Chicago, and had met her husband when they'd both been marching to protest a particularly usurious loan company that exploited poor blacks. She'd come from money and prominence but had betrayed her class, as it was often put in those days. She'd worked hard to get her husband elected, first to the House and then to the Senate. The Washington gentry hadn't liked her. Too liberal. But then, so was her husband.

Then she died, and after two years of loneliness he met Natalie, and while she hadn't changed him radically at first, he soon enough became unrecognizable to his old friends. He became interested in becoming wealthy, and if you can't become wealthy holding a Senate seat, then you are incompetent beyond repair. I believe the term is "license to steal" and that applies to both sides. Natalie was his unindicted co-conspirator. She was the darling of the lobbyists; she understood how secret deals were made to fill the coffers. I tried to imagine Natalie reading Saul Alinsky. I couldn't help myself. I laughed out loud.

"Do you talk to yourself, too?" Natalie had come in.

As I put the book back on the shelf, I said, "Yes, I do, and I find myself pretty damned interesting."

"I checked with Ben. That one radio interview still hasn't been rescheduled. You're supposed to do what I tell you to."

I turned to her and said, "Supposedly you hired us because we know more about campaigning than you do."

"We'll see how you feel when I stop payment on the very large check Winnie mailed to your firm today."

By now she was inside the room. At first she'd been addressing me from the doorway as if getting closer might cause her to be ill. She wore silver lamé lounging pajamas — trashy chic. She carried a martini in her left hand and a good deal of malice in her eyes. "I want you to leave."

Why waste time? "How much did Monica Davies want from you to keep quiet about Susan?"

You could never quite forget that she was an actress, not a great one but one who understood some of the basic skills of the craft. And this she did well — rolled her eyes and smiled. "Oh, God, you're really going to try and bail yourself out with this kind of bullshit?"

"Larson told me it was a lot of money."

I had the pleasure of watching the word "Larson" have the effect of a bullet between the eyes. "What the hell are you talking about?" The acting wasn't so good this time.

"He doesn't want his firm to be associated with blackmail. And I don't blame him.

171

So before the story breaks he wants to know what's going on. And so do I."

She walked past me, headed for the fireplace. At any other time I would assume that she wanted me to admire her body in the silver lamé pajamas. This time she was just stalling. We were well past the point where she'd ever care about me finding her seductive.

When she reached the chairs in front of the fireplace, she said, not turning around, "You may as well sit down."

"I'll stand."

She finished her martini and walked halfway back to me. Her years showed now, and they were cruel years. Winnie was so much more appealing than she'd ever be. Natalie wouldn't be able to fathom how that would be possible.

"I did it for Susan's sake."

"That's a lie. You did it so there'd be a Cooper in the House and eventually in the Senate. You did it for yourself, not for Susan."

"I've done a whole lot of things for Susan, and the bitch will never be grateful for them. I tried very hard to be her friend. I knew I'd always be her stepmother and nothing more. But some stepmothers and their daughters get on very well. Not her.

She wouldn't have any of it. She hated me from the day I came into this house. You should have seen her at our wedding. She would barely speak to me. Everybody saw it. It was humiliating. She idealized her mother, that was the problem. Her mother was this grand lady who gave herself to helping the poor. And I was this slut — she actually called me that more than once. This slut. She said I was corrupting her father."

She set her martini glass on a small table. She was performing, but at least the writing was getting better. "When I met John and saw all the opportunities he'd passed up, I wanted to help him. I'd been in Washington a few years by then and I knew a lot of people. He had this big house and this reputation as a reformer, but he didn't have all that much money. And times were changing. He'd come into office when the liberals dominated. But then things turned around, got very conservative. Susan always says that I made him change his votes. Well, if I hadn't, he never would have been elected for his last term — maybe not for his last *two* terms. And so he started traveling in conservative circles. We both did. We met a lot of different people. I'll grant you they were people he wouldn't have liked before, but he'd mellowed. And he became friendly with them."

All this was reverie; I wondered if she'd forgotten I was here.

"I need to know about the blackmail."

"Well, you can blame that bitch for that."

She was back at the dry bar then, fixing herself another martini. She talked as she worked. "We sent her to Smith. She stayed two years and then ran off to Paris. And then she traipsed all over the world. The worst part was when she came back to the States. The people she took up with — she was always getting into some kind of scrape. John was beside himself. That was when he developed sleeping problems. I'd find him in the middle of the night sitting up and staring at the wall. I always knew who he was thinking about. Worrying about."

"The blackmail. Tell me about the blackmail."

She sipped what she'd created. She turned it into stage business, pursing her lips as if she were a wine taster considering the latest offering, then came around from the bar, toting her glass, and said, "I didn't know about any of this until recently, when Monica Davies contacted me."

"Know about any of what?"

"I'm coming to that."

She seated herself with great style, setting

her drink on the arm of the leather chair. "You really should sit down, Dev. This may take a while."

"Not if you get to the point."

"The point, dear, is that my sweet little stepdaughter Susan slept around a lot."

"So?"

"And she didn't always sleep with the best sort of men. I always wondered if the thugs she dragged home were for my sake — to upset me, to rub my face in it. Her father was more understanding. He always sided with her and said that I was being a snob."

"And the point is what?"

"The point is that over the years there were two of them who later on tried to blackmail her. Threatened to go to the tabloids when Susan announced that she was running for Congress. I insisted she let me handle them, and I did. I hired a private detective and he found out that they were both on parole — if that tells you anything about the kind of man she was seeing — and he told them he would turn his files about them over to their respective parole officers immediately if they didn't cease and desist."

"And did they?"

"Of course. What choice did they have? But then Monica Davies came along."

"When did this start?"

"We were in Chicago at a regional convention and Davies was there. She took me aside at a cocktail party and whispered a name to me. The name didn't mean anything to me at the time. But she said to ask Susan about the man. That she'd tell me all about him. So naturally I did. And I had the great pleasure of seeing my stepdaughter start to come apart. All her haughtiness and arrogance — gone, just like that. In fact, she looked sick to her stomach when I started questioning her. At the time I didn't know anything about the man, but when Davies came back to me and started demanding money, she filled me in about him. A terrible, terrible person."

"Am I supposed to guess his name?"

"His name is Craig Donovan."

I walked over to the leather chair facing hers and sat on the arm. "Obviously Donovan went to Monica with his story. Monica would do the blackmailing because she was a lot more dangerous than he was — you knew that. You knew how ruthless she was. And she could destroy Susan overnight. So she cut Donovan in for a piece of it. Then she let you and Susan know what she wanted."

She lifted the martini to her mouth but

not before offering me a coy smile. "Very good. You should have been a private detective yourself, Dev."

"I'm smart enough to know that Susan has a son named Bobby Flaherty and that Bobby's in town with his young wife."

"Goddammit," she said. She made fists of her tiny hands and squeezed her eyes shut as if trying to will me out of existence. "This is all coming apart."

"I don't know what the hell you're paying them for."

The eyes were open now and they blazed at me. "You're not very smart after all. A child she gave up for adoption. A sleazebag like Craig Donovan the father. How would that look when the press got hold of it?"

"It wouldn't look good. But it could be explained. Bobby was born twenty years ago. Susan can make the case that she was in no condition to be a mother. She and Bobby are getting close now. I could see them at a joint press conference talking about all this."

"Oh, right. Can you imagine what Duffy would do with this?"

"It's better than living at the mercy of a blackmailer. And it'll come out eventually anyway. You've got several people involved, and that's a sure way of some reporter picking it up."

"What if Donovan goes on TV? Just putting him in front of a TV camera would damage her. I only met him once, but everything about him was sinister. Susan really did like slumming. And again I always thought it was another one of her childish ways of getting back at me."

"How was the money delivered?"

"Wyatt handled it. He's a very dutiful husband. He arranged for the money in the first place. Even for us, putting a quarter of a million dollars in cash is difficult. He put it in a large black briefcase with a lock on it. A combination lock. And took it to Monica Davies's hotel room. She took it. She offered him a drink, but he said he'd never drink with anybody like her."

"Did he think anybody else was in her room?"

"I asked him that myself. He said that he told her he needed to use her bathroom so he could look around. But he didn't see anybody."

"Was it a suite?"

"I asked him that, too. He said no. That's why he was pretty sure there wasn't anybody else there. There weren't many places to hide." She put her hands over her face and then took them down. "What're we going to

178

do, Dev?"

"I'm not sure yet. I need to learn a few more things."

"I'm just terrified it'll leak out somehow. All the stories about her wild-child days will be back in the news again. She won't have a chance."

It was time to go. "I'd appreciate you letting that check go through. I'd hate to have to sue you."

She was on her feet and standing two inches from me. "Oh, Dev, you know my temper. I say a lot of things I don't mean when I'm angry. Of course the check will go through. And, of course, you're not fired. I need you now more than ever."

I was tired of her and her devious charms. "I can find my way out. And I'd like to talk to Wyatt before I go."

"Wyatt's playing golf. Just keep me informed." She waved her dismissal. "Winnie's around somewhere. She'll see you out."

She was right about Winnie. I was no more than ten feet from the study when Winnie appeared and fell into step with me.

"You missed a good one in there. Acting class. Every fake emotion you could think of."

"Oh, now, weren't you at least a bit

179

charmed, Mr. Conrad?"

"Afraid not."

"I've seen her win over some very powerful men."

"Not anybody I'd care to know."

At the door she said: "There's more to her than you might think."

"There'd have to be. Nobody could be that superficial."

"Well, I guess I'll have to put you in the loss column."

"Loss column?"

She touched her fingers to her temple. "I keep a running score of who she's able to win over and who she's not. I'm afraid you're in the loss column."

"What's the score now?"

She smiled as she opened the door and held it for me. "You're her only loss."

"I'm proud of myself."

She touched my sleeve. "Between us, I'm proud of you, too. Now good-bye, Mr. Conrad."

I went back to the office and found David Manning using one of our phones. His face was red and his voice was sharp. "I've told you. Everything is fine with us. Very happily married. I don't know how many times I have to say it. Now I'm very busy."

As he spoke, his assistant, Doris Kelly, watched him. She was seated on the edge of the small divan where staffers relaxed sometimes. Her hands were tight little fists and her knuckles bone white.

"Look," Manning said into the phone, "I'm sorry I snapped at you. It's just that you're about the tenth caller in the past couple of hours. You're just doing your job and I should understand that. But I'm telling you the truth, all right?" Pause. "Thanks for saying that. I appreciate it." Pause. "You, too. Bye."

Away from Natalie and his servitude Manning was a competent, collected man. As he started to speak his eyes met Doris's. "I'll bring you up to date, Dev. There was a scene this morning. Natalie called. She wanted to see me. Urgent. I canceled a meeting so we could talk. I had a sense of what she was going to say, but it was still a shock. She came to my office and told me that a reporter had stopped her assistant Winnie and was asking questions about Susan and me — about our marriage and whether we slept in the same room. All those things. So then Natalie managed to track down Susan and demand that she come over to the office, too."

He stood up. His anger was harsh in his

eyes and voice. "Then when Susan came, Natalie told us that we need to start being seen in public together. Then Natalie got crazy. Everybody was shouting. There was a reporter in the lobby. I doubt she could hear the exact words, but she certainly heard all the anger."

"I don't like the sound of that, either," I said. "Did you hear any of it, Doris?"

"Yes. I have a small office outside of David's. I'm his receptionist, among other things."

"She's everything, Dev. I'm the most disorganized man on the planet. I couldn't get along without her." He nodded to Ben. "I just needed to get out of the office. So I came over here to tell you folks what happened. That reporter must have filed a story about it already because that was another reporter who called me here."

"We have to be at the college in twenty minutes, David."

Manning smiled down at Doris and said, "See what I mean about how she keeps me organized?"

After they were gone, Ben said, "I'll start working on a press release."

I went to one of the computers and started checking every local news source I could find. One newspaper, four radio stations.

Two of them carried stories of an angry exchange between Congresswoman Cooper and her stepmother.

"Two sources have the story, Ben."

"Everybody over at the Duffy campaign is probably drinking champagne and snorting coke and fucking each other's brains out."

"Let's go join 'em."

He held up a hand. "I don't want to smile."

"All right."

He laughed. "You're right. If we could catch Duffy all coked up and hitting on some seventeen-year-old volunteer . . ."

"Dream on."

He went back to banging out the press release. Hunched over his computer, his tie askew, a yellow pencil behind his ear, he looked like a reporter for a big-city newspaper of the forties or fifties, one of those hard-nosed guys in a film noir. He was one of the few people I knew who could write and talk at the same time. "That Doris. I always go for those kinds of looks. The sexy librarian. But I could never get near anybody who looks like her. I think there are certain types who are attracted to certain other types. And whatever her type is, my type doesn't do it for her." He blew out a breath. "I'm babbling."

"Gee, I hadn't noticed."

He paused long enough to flip me the bird. Then: "I'll finish this release and get a couple reporters over here and we'll talk it through. We have to answer it. 'All campaigns have spirited moments and this was just one of ours.' I'll make the argument about campaign tactics and say it didn't have anything to do with the marriage."

I spent the next half hour working on the campaign. I'd recently seen a documentary about my chosen profession. The script made an interesting point early on. Political campaigns have been with us for centuries, dating back to when a segment of Greeks had pushed to banish or kill Socrates. They had tried to discredit and smear him and it had worked. Political parties today did the same thing with less dire consequences. What I studied now were pages of microtargeting, a breakdown of key voting blocs we needed to win over, and how to tailor everything from our direct mail to our billboards to appeal to them.

We were headed into the final push, and that meant our TV and radio expenditures would quadruple. Not only did we have to create commercials that did us good, we had to create commercials that did us no harm. In every election cycle there is a story of a commercial or a series of commercials that damages the candidate who created them. You then spend your time, your desperate frantic time, trying to undo what you've done. This happens most often when you've made negative charges that are so nasty even some of your supporters find them unacceptable.

I wanted to know which segments we were still having trouble with. Duffy was a hard-liner but not a fool. He ran a careful, persuasive campaign that appealed to voting segments across the board. His chief vulnerability was that he'd been a lobbyist for twenty years before moving back to his hometown and running for office. We were happy to remind voters that he had worked as a hired gun for some pretty odious people and corporations, including one that had replaced local workers with a large number of undocumented ones. We'd decided early on to keep body-punching him with his history. By contrast we reminded voters of how much Susan had done for her district. We'd always known the race would tighten, and the internals we were seeing bore that out. We still had a safe lead. The task now would be to keep it.

Ben finished his press release and we went over it. We acknowledged that there had been a "discussion" between campaign staffers that had gotten heated, but then, "What campaign doesn't have heated discussions now and then?" We could deny that it had ever happened, that somebody had made up this "fight" story to discredit us, but that would only keep the incident alive. The press would push harder and harder to make us admit the truth. This way, with any luck, they'd quote our release and go on to something else.

The other staffers were gone. Lunch hours were staggered and there was work to do all over the district. During all this Kristin was in and out. She'd asked me twice if I knew where Susan was. There was another radio interview show she was supposed to be doing later this afternoon. I couldn't help her, of course. The final time she hurried back into the office she said: "She just called me on my cell."

I swiveled around in the chair. "Susan, you mean?"

"Right. She said she'd call the station at four and would do the interview."

"Did she say where she was?"

"No."

"Great."

Her gaze moved from me to Ben and back to me. "Do I get to know what's going on here? Why wouldn't Susan tell me where she was?"

"I don't know."

She glanced at Ben. "He's lying, isn't he?"

"I can't tell. He won't tell me what's going on, but maybe he doesn't know where she is."

"This whole thing is coming apart, isn't it?"

"Kristin —"

"Don't play that 'Kristin' bullshit, Dev. What's going on? You're the boss, but Ben and I are running this campaign. We asked you to deal with Susan only because you seem to be able to get along with Natalie. We deserve to know what the hell is going on."

Ben said, "I agree, Dev. I'd say if you don't trust us enough to tell us what you've found out, then why did you hire us in the first place?"

"Maybe I'll just go get drunk and call you later."

"Ben and I will go with you. We'll get you so bombed you'll tell us everything."

"Susan's name may come up in the Monica Davies murder."

"My God. Are you serious?"

"No, Kristin, I'm making it up because I enjoy watching you and Ben go into shock."

"You don't mean she actually committed the murder?" Again she glanced at Ben.

"I don't have any way of knowing. But my guess is no."

I spent ten minutes laying it out for them. The motel with the blood on the desk. Gwen and Bobby. Larson. The blackmail.

"And you don't know anything about this red-haired man — this Craig Donovan?" Ben said.

"He's Bobby's father. You see the resemblance to Susan when you look closely at Bobby. But he doesn't look like either one of them to any great degree."

"So what the hell are we going to do now?" Kristin said.

"There's only one thing to do," I said. "Find Donovan and confront him."

"How do you find him?"

"I'll have to lean on somebody I don't want to."

They stood beside me while I made my next phone call.

The Stay-Rite was a grim little motel on the north edge of Aldyne. It made the place where Gwen and Bobby had been staying look upscale. Two long flanks fanned out from a central office in standard fashion. The white stucco exterior looked as if a giant had pissed on it, long ugly streaks of rust covering much of the surface. In spots the walkway in front of the rooms had been reduced to rubble. One window bore a poster of Toby Keith and a few showed Confederate flags. The motel must have had rates for lengthy stays.

I'd learned about the place when I'd called Gwen from the office.

"Is Bobby there?"

"He's taking a shower."

"Good. I need to know where I can find Craig Donovan."

"Oh, God, Mr. Conrad, I can't tell you that. Bobby would never forgive me."

"I'm trying to help Bobby, Gwen, whether he knows it or not. You know that, don't you?"

She hesitated and then said, "Please never tell him I told you."

So here I sat on the edge of an industrial zone. The streets were lined with food franchises, tattoo parlors, convenience stores, and strip malls that looked like they'd been lifted from third-world countries.

I didn't know how I was going to handle it. This was the man with all the answers, and I didn't much care how I got them.

The sun was behind the clouds. The

afternoon had a faint scent of winter on it. Dog shit, what appeared to be dried human vomit, and the stain from a broken bottle of tomato juice covered the walk in front of room 146. Jagged pieces of glass looked like piranha teeth. Welcome home.

A game show played behind the faded red metal door. A female voice shouted, "Go for it, you stupid bitch! Go for it!" I had to knock loudly to be heard.

If you were drunk and forlorn enough, you might take her home when the bar announced last call for the night. She was maybe thirty and pretty in a ruined way. The breasts were balloons trapped inside a yellow terrycloth halter. The exposed belly was fleshy but not unattractive. The lower legs were shapely but the thighs were heavy. The red-and-blue cobra tattoos that climbed both her arms were nicely done. The teeth showed a heavy tobacco habit. And her right eye was her spiritual résumé. Somebody had punched her very hard and recently. She was a floozy. The hand on the hip, the cock of the head, the insolence of the brown gaze. "Who're you supposed to be?"

I smiled at the way she'd said it. "Well, I'm supposed to be a doctor. That's what my folks wanted. But it didn't turn out that way. Who're you supposed to be?"

"If it's any of your business, I'm supposed to be cutting hair at my sister's beauty shop right now, but she's such a bitch, I can't stand to be around her. So what do you want?"

"I'm looking for a man named Craig Donovan."

"Yeah? Why?"

"I have a message for him."

"I'm beginning to think you're a cop. I hate cops."

"Not a cop. Just a private citizen with a message."

The insolence was now anger. "You're lucky he isn't here. He'd punch your face in."

"The same way he punched yours in?"

Her stubby fingers touched her eye. The wound was fresh enough that she winced. "He didn't mean it."

"He mustn't have meant it when he put those bruises on your arm and neck, either."

Her cheeks colored. "Maybe I had it coming. I got a little drunk and I was talking to this guy at the bar while Craig was in the john and —" Then: "Why the hell am I telling you anything? This isn't any of your business. Now, get out of here before he comes back."

"Think he'll kick you around a little more

191

if he sees me here?"

"It'd be worth it just to see him pound your face in. Now go."

Behind her the phone rang. She traipsed back to it. Her bottom had survived her years. Nice and tight. She picked up and said, "Well, I can't fucking help it how busy you are. I've got the flu. I already told you that and I can't come in." Pause. "Well, what difference does it make if I'm sick in my apartment or sick over here?" Pause. "Well, you go right ahead and think I'm shacked up if you want. But I won't be in until I feel better."

She slammed the phone down and came back. "My sister's a real bitch. She runs this beauty parlor down the street. She treats me worse than any of her other beauticians. They have a day or two off, she don't say anything. I take a few days off . . ."

I had no doubt that she was an ideal employee. She had a good attitude and seemed easy to get along with.

Behind her the TV crowd erupted. I wondered if the contestant had taken her advice and gone for it after all.

"My name's Dev Conrad. Tell him I work for Natalie Cooper and tell him that I'm staying at the Commodore Hotel." I reached into the inside pocket of my suit coat and pulled out a loose card. "My cell phone number's on there. Tell him to give me a call."

She snapped the card from my fingers and looked at it. Fear played in her eyes now. She swallowed hard. "When I give him this card he's going to say that you came into the room and I let you do something to me."

"Grab your clothes. I'll take you anywhere you want to go. I don't want to see you get hit anymore."

"For your information, I'm in love with him. He told me he'd marry me." She was beyond help again. "I'm not gonna spend my life working for my sister, that's for sure."

"What's your name?"

"Why?"

"Just like to know who I'm talking to."

"Heather, if it's any of your fucking business."

Somewhere in the ether the TV crowd had a collective orgasm.

She stepped back into the dank darkness of the room and slammed the door.

I was used to spending time with women who lived in apartments or condos. Chicago women mostly. It had been a long time since I'd pulled into a driveway and walked up to a door. Inevitably I thought of high-school days and facing parents in order to drag off their daughters for love or something like it. Even in your forties those memories are vivid. Too many of them were like opening night in front of a hostile audience. I always had to writhe through small talk while trying to seem as harmless as possible. *Yes, sir, I promise to get your daughter home at nine-thirty, and with her virginity still intact.*

At least Jane didn't have a father on the premises. She opened the door in a rush of smiles and perfume and a small hand that squeezed one of mine. She wore a black wrap dress that emphasized her slender hips and small but most intriguing breasts. Her red beaded necklace matched the color of her lipstick. "This is exciting. A real date."

Behind her in the vestibule two mutt cats — one golden tom and one black-and-white female — stood primly watching us. She turned to them and said, "Now you've got plenty of food and water. And I've left the TV on for you in the family room. I'll see you later."

As she was locking the door, she said, "It's pathetic how I talk to them. But when my marriage started going south I guess they became the kids we never quite got around to having."

"I've got a cat of my own in Chicago. She has my power of attorney."

On the way to the restaurant she'd selected, she spent a few minutes trying to find a station that played old standards. "It's funny. I love a lot of the music today, even some of the rap. But when I want to feel like a grownup, I like Sinatra and Tony Bennett and people like that."

"You like rap?"

"I said 'some of it.' I had my twelve-year-old niece with me this summer for a month. Her folks are going through a divorce and we've always been close, so she came out here from Connecticut to get away from everything at home. I couldn't believe how much rap she listened to. A very upper-class white girl. Anyway, I guess she wore down my defenses. There are three or four rap songs I actually enjoy."

The restaurant was tucked into some pines. There were so many Beemers, the parking lot resembled a dealership. The owner was also the greeter, an Aspen type, a big guy in a red flannel shirt, a black leather vest, and jeans. The Rolex on his right wrist spoiled the effect he wanted — a TV version of a cowhand — as did the capped teeth. There were two levels to the place — the enormous fireplace and bar

195

downstairs and the tall booths and tables on the second level. The waitress dressed pretty much like the greeter. She was young and sweet and probably couldn't afford a Rolex. While we waited for our drinks, Jane said, "If I start getting drunk, stop me. I'm an embarrassing drunk, believe me."

"I've been known to be pretty embarrassing myself."

"Did you ever get into fights?"

"Not when I was drunk. Sometimes when I worked in army intelligence but not very often."

"My soon-to-be ex thought he was a heavyweight champion when he got drunk. He was always picking fights. When he woke up the next morning I'd have to remind him of what he'd done."

"I've had too many of those nights myself."

"Did you drink a lot when you were married?" Then, "Damn."

"What?"

"I shouldn't have asked that question. It was stupid."

"Logical question given what we were talking about. And no, it wasn't the drinking; it was the fact that I spent so much time away from home working on campaigns. I wasn't faithful and neither was she. She had a good excuse for it. I didn't."

"Do you get along with her now?"

"I don't see her that often. My daughter says that she's very happy with her new husband. I'm glad for her. I was a selfish bastard. When I found out she had a lover, I got jealous and stupid. I ranted for days even though I'd pushed her into it."

"Maybe she would have been unfaithful anyway."

"Maybe. But the point is, I blamed her when I'd been unfaithful long before she was."

We started in on the warm bread hidden in a basket and wrapped in a heavy wine-red napkin. As she picked up the butter knife, she said, "I tried to be unfaithful one time. I found this note in his pocket from one of the secretaries where he works. It was obvious what was going on. I got dressed up and went out to a bar just the way women do in movies, and I sat at a little table and three or four men hit on me. I was never a beauty like Susan, but I did all right. And it was fun sitting there and flirting and feeling the way I did in college. But when it came down to going home with this guy — and he was really good-looking — I just couldn't do it. And it's not because I'm so moral or anything. We'd been married for eleven years and even when he was cheating — I guess I just didn't want to be like him. Does that make any sense?"

"Sure."

The salmon steaks were very good. We both drank Manhattans. The longer we talked the more I liked her, and in the candlelight her sensible good looks took on real beauty. I knew I was getting interested in her because I was starting to wonder what she thought of me as well.

"Are you dying to ask me about Susan?"

"Well, I thought I'd get around to it eventually."

"She called me." Her expression and her voice tightened. "I sounded flip just a moment ago. I shouldn't have. I'm really worried about her."

"What did she say?"

"Nothing new, really. But her tone of voice — really desperate. Something must have happened. This is just terrible for her. She's so afraid that the press will find out about Bobby before she's ready to talk to them about it. It doesn't help that Natalie keeps trying to control everything. Natalie still believes she can contain this thing. That sure doesn't help Susan any. I've told her that I can't see how this will be such a terrible scandal. She put her boy up for adoption. She didn't abort him. And he got a much better home environment than she could have given him at the time. I guess I don't understand politics."

The waitress appeared and asked us about dessert. Neither of us was interested. I asked for the check.

"It's early yet," I said. "Would you like to go someplace else?"

"Not really. I'd rather just go back to my house. Maybe watch TV. Hopefully with you along."

"That sounds good. I just hope professional wrestling's on tonight."

She made a face. "Are you serious?"

"No," I said.

"God, you do deadpan very well. I thought, This guy likes professional wrestling?"

"I mostly watch old movies and talk shows."

"I get tired of all those talking heads. They think they're so important."

"You noticed that, huh?" I said as I signed the MasterCard form.

A few minutes later we were walking through the night to my rental. Jane leaned against me. I had my arm around her shoulders. The parking lot had been full, so we'd had to slide into the lone slot in the narrow drive of the business next door, right on the edge of the adjacent loading dock.

She'd tucked herself into me as we walked. Her head came just to my chest and I could smell clean hair and light perfume. She felt good there. Comfortable. I was looking forward to going back to her house. I didn't think I'd be spending the night, but I was sure we'd know each other a lot better by the time I left. My daughter was always urging me to meet somebody. Maybe I had.

There was little light and that made it all the easier for him. As I leaned over to unlock her door, he ran at me and leapt on my back. I didn't even have time to turn around. He honored the verities of an earlier era. He wore brass knuckles and he hit me hard enough and fast enough that I was on the ground before Jane could even start screaming. Elapsed time was seconds.

He stank of sweat, whiskey, and after-shave. As I twisted around I got a glimpse of red hair and a pair of insane blue eyes. I was aware of Jane trying to pull him off me. He somehow flung her away with such force that she fell over backward. I heard her crash on the concrete. She was still screaming.

I was on my hands and knees, trying to get my footing, fighting through the pain from the pounding my head had taken.

"Tell that bitch the price is double now, Conrad. I want another payment of the same amount by eight o'clock tomorrow night. You understand that?"

I found my rage. I came up off the ground so fast that I surprised him. I slammed into him with such force that he had to struggle to stay upright. I was all fists and fury. The biggest problem I had was my vision. All the brass punches had taken their toll. My vision was gauzy. I was still swinging at him, but he'd moved back and I was starting to stumble.

I heard Jane behind me. Running toward me. "He's got a gun, Dev!"

And so he had. Later on it would have a strange humor for me. Brass knucks and a gun. Susan Cooper sure had picked a sweetie pie.

Between my failing eyesight and my pain, he didn't need his gun to make sure I was no threat. He just lunged forward and shoved me. Not even rage could keep me upright. I slumped against the rental. I could hear him running away, but it was just sensory data. I was too weak to care.

I started to slide down the side of the rental. Then Jane had her arms around me. "I'm going to get you in the car, and then

I'm driving us to the hospital."

"No, no hospital."

"What? He could've killed you!"

I was having a hard time swallowing. "Your place. Your place."

I leaned away from the car so I could open the passenger door. I managed to crawl inside and lay my head back against the seat. I don't know whether I passed out or just went to sleep. It didn't matter. I was out.

Strange room, strange clothes, strange memories. Moonlight through a window, silver and shadowed. I lay on a bed in a pair of pajamas I'd never seen before. My own animal smells; my own animal contours as I stretched. There was pain, and with the pain came memories. The parking lot and the brass knuckles and the gun. Three bumps on the left side of my head. The impulse to get out of bed was slowed by the fact that I was dizzy. I had to move carefully. I didn't even try to stand up at first. Just sat on the edge of the bed. I needed a bathroom and then I needed some coffee. A fragment of fantasy — me beating Craig Donovan to death. His face bloody, his eyes pleading as I sent him into the darkness.

The door opened. She was backlit and in

silhouette. "I thought I heard you."

"What time is it?"

"Just before four-thirty. You got about eight hours' sleep, anyway. How's your head feel?"

"How the hell did you get me into pajamas and then into bed?"

"I'm more resourceful than you realize."

"You'd have to be."

"But you didn't answer my question. How's your head?"

"Hurts. But I doubt it's anything serious."

"I went online and checked for the symptoms of a concussion. You didn't seem to have them, so I put you to bed. There's a bathroom right down the hall. I'll heat up some coffee. You be all right?"

"Yeah. And thanks for taking care of me."

"That's the most scared I've ever been in my life. I've never seen anything like that before. I wanted to kill him. Even as mad as I get at my ex, I never seriously think about killing him. But this guy —"

"Believe me, I've been thinking the same thing. I hope I get a chance to pay him back." Then: "I'll be all right. I'll see you in the kitchen."

"You sure you don't need help?"

"I'll be fine."

I knew I was feeling stronger. Something

like pride was keeping me from telling her that I was dizzy. I was beginning to realize that Donovan had hurt my ego far more than he'd hurt my body. Even though I hated all the macho bullshit that burdens most men, I didn't like the feeling of being helpless and at somebody else's mercy. Jane had seen how weak I was. I didn't want to stand up and fall down.

"You sure?" She didn't sound sure.

"I'll be fine. I'll see you in the kitchen."

After her silhouette vanished from the doorway, I stood up and stayed in place until the worst of the dizziness faded. Then I started the slow, careful process of getting to the bathroom. The cold water I splashed on my face brought me awake, the warm muzziness of the bed banished. I was pissed off. Oh, did I have plans for him. My anger overrode any pain I had. It was as if a TV minister had laid hands on me and I'd been reborn. I smiled at myself in the mirror for being such a clever bastard. At the moment my image of a TV minister seemed the wittiest thing I'd ever thought of. What a fine, swell, wonderful guy I was.

The smell of bacon and eggs lured me like a sea siren to my seat in a small nook by a line of casement windows. I would have bet I wasn't hungry.

Jane brought me a cup of coffee and said, "Food'll be ready in a few minutes."

I took her hand. "I owe you for this. Thanks very much."

She leaned down and kissed me on the cheek. "Well, look at it this way, Dev. You gave me the most memorable night of my sheltered life." She took her smile back to the stove and finished up our breakfast.

We went over everything again, of course. She still thought I should have called the police. But now that I was awake I began focusing on what Donovan had actually said about doubling the payment, and by eight o'clock tonight.

Jane said, "I wonder why Donovan came after you."

"I left my card with his girlfriend yesterday. He obviously thinks I'm the point man now — that I'm acting for Natalie."

"I keep wondering how Natalie's going to take it," she said. "You know, when you tell her Donovan wants another payment."

"I'm wondering the same thing."

"Do blackmailers usually do stuff like this?"

The conversation amused me suddenly. "Well, I looked it up in *Blackmailing for Dummies* and they said that it's always a possibility."

"*Blackmailing for Dummies.* You must have quite a library."

"I hope you get a chance to see it sometime."

"Boy, is Natalie going to be pissed. If I didn't love Susan so much, I could almost enjoy seeing Donovan treat Natalie like this."

Just then a jagged slice of pain cleaved my skull. I must have winced because Jane said, "Let me get some Tylenol."

I didn't argue.

When she came back, she served us breakfast and I swallowed the capsules. French toast, eggs, and bacon. I allowed myself to feel fat and lazy for a few minutes. But then the pain reminded me that I had things I needed to do.

"I need to go, Jane. The food — everything . . ." I rose and took a few steps toward her. I took her hand. "Thanks. I really owe you."

"You're leaving now?"

"It's almost five-thirty. I want to get ready to go see Natalie and Wyatt."

"Nuts," she said. And laughed. "My mother said that I was a very spoiled child and that that was my favorite word whenever I didn't get my way."

I took the linen napkin, dipped the edge

206

of it in her glass of water, and then wiped away a tiny button of egg yolk on the side of her lovely mouth.

"Oh, great," she said, "I'll bet that looked sexy, whatever it was."

I raised her gently to her feet. We were both in pajamas. As we kissed I felt her warm yielding body shifting against mine. I think we were both in a kind of trance as she led me back through the house. When we passed one door she said, "That's the master bedroom. Where I had to sleep with you-know-who. The guest room all right?"

"Fine."

And it was fine indeed.

I walked into the headquarters' office at 6:47. Ben was already there drinking coffee from a large McDonald's container and studying his computer screen with enough concentration to levitate it. Without looking up he said, "Couldn't sleep. Kristin called me late last night and said she was at a club where a reporter told her there'd be a big story about internal problems in our campaign." Then: "By the way, you're off the hook. She told me she met this guy last night and she's in love."

I took my own McDonald's coffee container to the desk I'd been using. "I take it the story ran."

"Yeah and it's long. I haven't finished it yet."

I logged onto the newspaper Web site and started reading. I was only a quarter of the way through when my head started pounding again. Words could hit just as hard as Donovan's brass knuckles.

"I wonder how long this guy has been dating Duffy?" Ben said, referring to the reporter.

"It sure as hell reads like that, doesn't it?" The bastard had done a good job. The infighting between Susan and Natalie, how Natalie treated her staff, and citing four well-known and embarrassing moments from Susan's past.

"It doesn't get any worse than that," Ben said.

"The hell it doesn't."

I gave him a quick version of what had happened last night and Donovan's demand for a double payment. "The son of a bitch might do anything, Ben. That's the hell of it."

"He's a sadistic bastard."

I was on my feet again. "Now I have to go talk to Byrnes and Natalie." I walked over and picked up my coat.

"You remember any prayers?"

"Yeah."

"If I had to face Natalie, I'd say a whole lot of them."

■ ■ ■ ■

PART THREE

■ ■ ■ ■

CHAPTER 15

The grass on the endless lawn of the Cooper mansion glittered with frost that was only now beginning to dry off. As I pulled closer I could see that the flower beds had been covered. Except for a border collie sniffing at the base of a tree I didn't see anything moving around the place. As I passed the garage I noticed that all four of the doors were closed. I parked in front and took my time getting to the door. The cold air felt good, though the weather report said rain was expected by midafternoon.

Winnie answered the door. "They're just finishing breakfast. I'm sure there'll be plenty for you."

"No thanks. In fact, if you wouldn't mind, I wish you'd let me sit in the study and tell Wyatt I'd like to talk to him at his convenience." I'd decided to talk to Wyatt alone first. He'd never studied drama.

"You look very serious this morning."

213

"This is important, Winnie. All I can tell you is that the whole campaign is starting to come apart. I need to talk to Wyatt."

Behind her I heard Natalie's voice. "Winnie, why is the front door open? There's a draft in case you hadn't noticed." I could see past Winnie into the morning shadows of the hall that ran through the center of the house. Natalie was somewhere back there. "Did you hear me, Winnie? Now close that goddamn door."

"We have a caller, Natalie. Mr. Conrad is here."

"Here?" she snapped. "What the hell's he doing here?"

She came into the light like a heat-seeking missile, ready to hit her target. She wore a black dressing gown that had a train like a wedding dress. She came up to me like a punk ready to fight. She looked perfect. "Do you have any idea what time it is? And we don't receive visitors unless they call first."

Winnie had stepped aside as if afraid of violence.

"Natalie, I could give a shit about your rules. I want to talk to Wyatt in the study, and I don't want you in there with him. And I don't want you listening at the door."

I moved so fast she had to back up. She made noises that were not exactly words.

Finally she shouted, "Wyatt! I want you to call the police!"

A few seconds later Byrnes appeared, walking fast. He wore a Western shirt and jeans. His feet were bare. Before he reached us he said, "What the hell's going on?"

"I want him arrested."

"Oh, for God's sake, Natalie, what the hell are you talking about?" To me he said, "Why're you here so early?"

"Have you read the paper this morning or gone online?"

"No, why?"

"They're moving on us. Right now they're just talking about internal squabbling with our campaign. But obviously somebody in our camp is talking to this reporter. I'm pretty sure it's going to get a lot worse."

"You bastard," she said. "This is all your fault. You and Ben. I don't know why I ever hired you. You're the most incompetent people I've ever worked with." She stabbed a finger in my direction. "You're a fucking joke!"

It was a good exit line. She whipped her train around her and stalked to the sweeping staircase. She had learned her Scarlett O'Hara well.

Byrnes sighed and shook his head. "Well, you may as well come in. Natalie's already going to have my head anyway. Winnie, would you bring us coffee in the study?"

"Of course."

I followed him into the study. His bare feet slapped on the parquet floor. He was swearing under his breath the whole time.

When we were inside, he walked over to one of the mullioned windows and opened it from the bottom. He pointed to a leather wing chair. I sat and watched him dig something out of his desk. I wasn't sure what it was until he was standing next to the open window. He tamped a cigarette from a pack of Winstons. "My secret vice. I only smoke one when I'm really stressed. And this morning sure as shit qualifies. It's going to be hell around here." He stood by the window, exhaling into the fresh air. I half expected him to stick his head outside and smoke.

He took seven or eight drags, inhaling each of them. Then he licked his thumb and forefinger and squeezed the flame out between them. "My father taught me that trick. Picked it up when he was a cowboy — a real one, not a pretend one like me." He sounded bitter. He closed the window, locked it, and walked back to his desk.

But he wasn't done with the smoking ceremony yet. From a different drawer he pulled one of those small battery-powered fans. He turned it on. It sounded like the biggest horse fly that had ever lived. He went back to the window and began covering the entire area with swipes of the fan. Then he shut it off, brought it back to the desk, closed the drawer, and sat down.

"She hasn't caught me yet." His smile was sour. He was a prisoner of her wealth and power like everybody else. The stranglehold.

"I assume something bad has happened, Dev, or you wouldn't be here so early."

"Craig Donovan paid me a visit last night."

"What did that bastard want?"

"You mean aside from working on my head with brass knuckles?"

"I want to kill that son of a bitch. He swaggers in here and makes his demands. You can see how much he's enjoying himself. No matter how low Susan sank when she was running around, I don't know how she ever hooked up with him. He's a psychopath. I resented giving him a damned dime. But then it's not my money. Natalie thought she could buy him off the one time and he wouldn't come back for more."

"He's already come back for more."

"What the hell're you talking about?"

"He wants double the amount. Another

217

full payment."

"He's crazy."

"He probably is. But right now that doesn't matter. We have to figure out how to handle this."

I was surprised he didn't go for another cigarette. His face tried to form an expression that contained both anger and misery. He just looked helpless. "Natalie's going to hit the roof."

"The threat is he goes public. The trouble is that if you pay him twice he may ask for even more."

"Goddammit," he said. "I always think of myself as a man of the world. I've been around the block more than a few times, Dev. I've even heard of people being shaken down like this. But they agreed to pay and they were left alone for a while. Donovan's a wild man. Who the hell knows what he's going to do?"

"There's always the chance he's bluffing."

"You believe that's the case?"

"I don't have any idea. He's too unpredictable."

There wasn't any doubt who was pounding on the door. There had been our quiet conversation and now there was a threatening thunder of assaults on the wood that was keeping her out.

He shook his head. "It's not locked, Natalie."

"I want to know exactly what you're talking about. This is my house and my money being spent, and whether this bastard likes it or not I have the final say on this campaign."

So nice to see you, Natalie. Won't you have a cup of coffee and sit down and chat for a while? You just have a way of brightening up a room.

She charged up to Byrnes's desk. "What the hell have you two been talking about?"

"Darling, it would help if you'd calm down."

"This bastard forces his way in here at breakfast time and I don't know what's going on — in my own house? Now I want to hear everything you've said."

And with that she gathered her black train and went to sit in a leather wing chair identical to mine. I took pleasure in watching her try to get comfortable with her ridiculous train piled beneath her. She was angry with her train. If she got mad enough at it, she'd probably set it on fire.

Byrnes sighed and said, "You won't be happy to hear this, Natalie."

"And why should that make any difference? I haven't been happy to hear anything since this man and his flunkies started bungling Susan's campaign."

"This isn't something they did, Natalie. This is —"

I could almost see him drawing himself up to give her the bad news. "Craig Donovan physically attacked Dev last night and told him that he wanted a second payment in the same amount — and he wants it delivered by tonight."

Both Byrnes and I were ready to crouch into defensive positions because the blast would likely smash windows and toss furniture around. But it didn't happen. We glanced at each other. It was a cartoon moment, when two characters stare at a stick of dynamite that burns down but doesn't explode.

She laughed. "Well, isn't that just fucking ducky? So now Mr. Conrad here has managed to screw up the situation with Donovan, too." The voice started to rise at the end. "And just why the hell did he come to you?"

I lied. "I'm not sure."

"That doesn't matter now. What matters is what we do next. Do we pay him again?"

She put her head down, folded her hands in her lap, and began shaking her head back and forth. Without looking up she said, "If we weren't so close to the election, I'd fire your ass and rip you up in public, which I plan to do whether we win or lose." This was the old Natalie. She didn't want to disappoint her fans. When her head came up she glared at Byrnes. "If you were any kind of a man, you'd punch him right in the face."

"Oh God, Nat," Byrnes said. "C'mon. That kind of talk isn't going to help anything."

"Oh? And just what kind of talk *will* help anything?"

He started to push back from his desk. I had the same impulse he did. To get up and walk around, anything to break the tension.

"Why don't I fix you a brandy, Nat?" Byrnes said.

"It's eight o'clock in the goddamned morning, Wyatt. What are we, lushes?" But her words lacked their usual fire. She sounded more miserable than angry. When she finally met my eyes, she said, "I want you out of here."

"All right."

"I'm going to fix it so you'll have a hard time getting any kind of clients, Conrad — even city council ones. I'll ruin you." Then to Byrnes: "I thought you were going to get me a brandy? You don't do anything else around here. Can't you at least do that?"

There was no point in saying good-bye. I was at the moment in crime movies of the forties when the detective always picks up his fedora and walks out. Except I didn't have a fedora. I closed the door quietly.

About halfway down the hall, just at the point where I could see the sunlight blaze through the vestibule window, Winnie appeared and slid her arm through mine. "I take it Natalie's not happy."

"I don't know how you stand it."

Her laugh was warm and bright. "Oh, Natalie's all right. In her way she means well. She's like most control freaks. They think they're doing you a favor by having everything their own way. It's for your own good — and they just don't understand why you can't understand that. I had an older sister who was like that, God rest her soul."

She opened the front door for me. The chill, brilliant day leapt at me. She looked back down the hall. "There are times when I actually feel sorry for her."

I smiled. "I guess I haven't gotten to that point yet. And somehow I don't think I ever will."

She touched my arm and laughed. "A lot of people say that, I'm afraid." Then she was closing the door, sealing herself inside

the tomb with the one and only Natalie
Cooper.

CHAPTER 16

David Manning and Doris Kelly sat next to each other just inside the office headquarters. Given their expressions you'd think they were patients waiting on bad news from a doctor.

Manning said, "We're hiding out here, Dev." Doris nodded. She was pale and nervous.

"From what?"

Before Manning could speak, Ben came back from his desk and said, "They got it after we did."

"Got what?"

"Reporters," Ben said. "Three of them were here for an hour. I had to practically push them out the door. Then they went over to the foundation."

"That's why we came over here," Manning said.

From her desk, Kristin said, "Then they started in on me first."

"What the hell are we all talking about?" I said.

"The son. Bobby," Ben said. "Somehow they found out about Susan and her son."

So there you had it. The information hit my brain and my entire body tensed. The word was out and from here on in there was no way we could get ahead of this story. All we could do was defend ourselves, and when you defend yourself a good share of people assume you're guilty. If we'd broken the story at a press conference that we had called, we could have spun it our way — a mother re united with her son, sad and sorry that she'd had to give him up for adoption, but now they were together again. Duffy and the press would still have come after us, but at least we would have put a tender face on it before the savagery began.

"I assume we don't know who contacted the press."

"Not yet, Dev," Ben said.

Manning said, "We've got a lot of work to do at the foundation, but I don't want to go back there. I don't want to get trapped into saying the wrong thing."

"They even followed me to the bathroom," Doris said. "I was half afraid the woman reporter was going to follow me inside."

"I suppose Duffy'll be on TV right away.

Gloating."

"He won't have to be on TV, David," I said. "The press'll do all his work for him. He can stay above it. He gets to sit in the stands while we get ripped up in the arena."

"Who the hell knew about it?" Ben said. "Just a handful of people."

"Larson, that's who I'm thinking of." Kristin continued working on her computer as she talked. "That's what he's good at. He manages to find out things that other people never get to."

I was thinking of the woman I'd met at Craig Donovan's. Another possibility. She knew about it. Donovan would have told her. Not unthinkable that he'd beaten her again and she'd decided to ruin his plan for blackmail.

The first thing I had to concentrate on was preparing a presentation for the press. I had to find Susan and we had to work out a story. Then we had to find Bobby. Even though our heartwarming mother-and-son reunion spin was late, it had to be performed, anyway. We had to do our best to keep Susan in a sympathetic light. We would lose votes over this; the thing was to hold those losses to a minimum.

"I need to talk to Susan," I said. "What's her schedule today?"

"She doesn't have anything until late this afternoon," Kristin said.

"Where is she now?"

Kristin shrugged. "I don't know, Dev."

I tried her cell phone number. No answer. "When was the last time anybody talked to her?"

Manning said, "I managed to get her when the reporters started coming. I think she was out at Jane's."

I grabbed a phone book from a nearby desk and searched for Jane's number. I punched the digits in. Jane answered. "How're you feeling?"

"Pretty good. Jane, is Susan there?"

The phone seemed to go dead. "Jane?"

"I can't answer that."

"You just did answer it. I need to talk to her. I'm sorry about putting you in the middle, but she's got to talk to me."

"We heard the news station. About Bobby."

"Please put her on."

"I'm not sure she'll talk to you — or anybody, Dev."

"Try. Please. She's a big girl. She's got to face this."

"She's scared."

"So are the rest of us."

"Damn," she said. "Just a minute, Dev.

I'll do what I can."

When she finally came on the phone, Susan said, "I don't think there's anything I can do except resign. I'm just trying to get up the nerve to call a press conference and get it over with."

"We need to talk."

"I just told you I'll need to resign."

Her words didn't surprise me. I'd seen this happen to politicians before. There are those who hang on forever. *Sure, I visited whorehouses every night for twenty years and took more than a million dollars in graft and have a fifteen-year-old girlfriend. But is that any reason to deprive my constituents of my brilliance?* At the other extreme you find those who just get overwhelmed and decide they don't have the strength they thought they had. They get tired, they get worn down, they get embarrassed, and they think, The hell with it. One painful press conference and they'll slink off the stage. Susan was in that mode now.

"Not before we talk. I need to know everything before we talk about resigning."

"This isn't your decision; it's mine."

"That's true. But maybe I can help you make the right one."

"You really think we still have a chance?"

"It's possible to put a good face on this,

Susan. If we think it through. You have a son. You've been reunited. You're about to become a grandmother."

"I guess that's why we pay you." Her laugh was weary. "I got a chill when you said 'grandmother.' I could see how it might work. I love Bobby and I love Gwen."

"Good. I'll see you in twenty minutes."

After I hung up, I saw them looking at me — Ben, Kristin, Manning, and Doris Kelly. Kristin was smiling. "You should write soap operas. You had me going there. I can really see how this could play at a press conference."

Doris Kelly said, "There was a lot more of that going on than anybody wanted to admit — giving children up for adoption when the mothers didn't know what else to do. I don't see where that would be such a big deal."

It wasn't the force of her idea that startled me; it was the fact that she'd expressed it. I'd never heard her really say anything before.

"This is a long way from over," Ben said.

"I'm going out to see Susan. You've got my cell number if you need to talk to me."

"What do you want to tell the press for now?" Kristin said.

"Tell them we'll be announcing a press

conference and until then we won't have anything to say."

"That's going to be some press conference," Ben said.

"It had better be, Ben. Or we're all through."

All the way out to Jane's I played a fantasy press conference in my mind. With Susan standing with Gwen and Bobby and presenting the whole thing as a happy story of reunion rather than any kind of scandal — and promises of being together from now on — we could create a reconciliation narrative that the press would go for. Interviews with Bobby about his growing-up years. Interviews with Gwen about what a fine man Bobby was and how the baby would bring them even closer together. David Manning would have to put in an appearance, too. Some camera time for all four of them, David, of course, delighted at this sudden surprise. I'd keep Natalie chained in a bunker somewhere. Duffy would keep going at us, but he'd have to be careful. These were no longer the days of *The Scarlet Letter.* These were the days of watching fame-driven nobodies giving blow jobs to other fame-driven nobodies right there on the family screen. They called them reality shows. Well, our show was G-rated compared to that kind of sleaze.

Jane met me at the front door. Given her somber appearance, there should have been a black wreath on the door and I should have been bearing condolences.

"Just go easy on her, Dev. She's really confused right now. And very vulnerable. She's a tough cookie and always has been. So seeing her this way is kind of scary."

I went inside. It seemed natural to pull her to me and give her a hug. It seemed even more natural to give her a kiss. She smelled good and tasted even better.

There was a coat tree in the vestibule. She pulled down a blue goose-down vest. "I'm going to do some grocery shopping. She's in the kitchen in the breakfast nook. She's had way too much coffee, too. There's plenty of caffeine-free diet Pepsi in there. Get her to drink that instead."

She gave me another hug and then left.

Susan wore a simple white shirt. Her hair was in a ponytail. The first glimpse I got of her she was biting one of her manicured nails.

"You're wasting a lot of money."

"What?"

At first her eyes didn't seem to focus. She had to bring them back from whatever terrible land she'd been visiting. "Wasting a lot of money?"

"You pay to get your nails done and then you're biting them."

"Oh." The smile was sad. "I guess you're right. Sort of ruins the whole effect, doesn't it?"

She lifted her cup.

"Jane thinks you've had enough coffee."

"God, I wouldn't make it through this without Jane. I'll switch to something else when I finish this."

I slid into my side of the booth. On the other side of the window the backyard was filled with Disney creatures — squirrels and birds and two small dogs playing in the dusty light of fall.

"How're Ben and Kristin taking it?"

"They think we can pitch our side and the majority of people will understand."

"Really?"

"We have to be careful how we present it, but we have enough time before the election to see it mostly go away. If —"

She stopped me. "If?"

"If Donovan doesn't up the ante again — or do something else."

"Oh, God, what did he do?"

I told her about last night and demanding another payment.

"He's the most devious person I've ever known — a sociopath who loves to play games. He'd blackmail people, and then when they paid him, he'd immediately demand more. Right on the spot. He told me he knew he couldn't get it; he just liked to see them suffer. He enjoys the torture as much as the money."

"That doesn't exactly surprise me."

She took a deep breath, exhaled. "This whole moment — I wish I could just enjoy the fact that I've been reunited with my son and his wife and that I'm going to be a grandmother. And poor Gwen, what she's going through —"

"We need to call a press conference for this afternoon. Three-thirty at the latest so we can get on all the evening news shows. This is going to be tough for you, but you've got to do it right."

"I don't want to go on television and lie, Dev."

"You won't be lying. You'll talk about how good it is to be reunited with your son and that you'll go into detail at a later date. If anybody brings up the fact that the police questioned him, just say that they've been questioning a lot of people, which they no doubt have." I didn't tell her about the great grand dream I'd had of her, Bobby, and sweet pregnant Gwen all together in front of the cameras. We were past that now; all we could do was get on the air as soon as possible and start controlling the message as best we could. No long-lost sons or winsome daughters-in-law for props.

"I'll run, that'll help. It always relaxes me."

"Run, shower, get dressed, and then spend some time with Ben and Kristin at the office. They'll know what to do. You'll be nervous when you see the reporters, but once you start talking you'll be fine. It's what you said awhile ago, how this should be a happy time for you. That's all you need to convey. The happy time. The family together again. Make a few jokes about being a grandmother at your age."

"You have a lot of faith in me. I hope I can do it." She sat back and looked at me. "The terrible thing is that I want to get reelected. All these other awful things going on all around me and I'm still thinking about my job."

"You're a good congresswoman. You enjoy your work and you're actually helping people. Nothing wrong with that."

A bittersweet smile. "Poor Natalie. She'll probably have to be sedated by the time this is all over."

"That's a nice thought," I said. "Natalie

234

Cooper — sedated."

As I slid out of the booth, I said, "I'll check in with Ben in an hour or two."

She held out her hand. I took it. Ice cold. "Maybe I'm the one who needs to be sedated, Dev."

CHAPTER 17

Peter Cooper didn't like me because I'd rejected his speeches. I didn't expect a warm welcome and I didn't get one.

Mandy Gilmore, his secretary, had accompanied Peter on a visit to my office a few months ago. She hadn't liked me much that time, and now that I'd declined to use his speeches she liked me even less. She was on her headset when I opened the door. She was also riffling through some papers. She started to look up, the automatic smile already in place. When she recognized me she flipped the friendly greeting switch off instantly. She pointed to one of the green leatherette-covered chairs beneath the map of Susan's district.

I went over and sat down and tried not to listen to her. She turned away and muttered something that contained one word I understood: "Asshole." I was pretty sure who she was referring to.

After she hung up she gave me a sharp look and said, "I know you don't believe in appointments, but that's how we do things around here."

Today she wore a frothy amber blouse and a dark skirt. She would have been attractive if she'd ever let go of her anger. But she'd found a way to channel all the sorrows of her life into her gatekeeper job, and the sullenness was taking its toll.

"I know he's here. I saw his car. I need to talk to him now. If you won't tell him I'm here, then I'll walk over to his door and tell him myself."

"You're a real bastard, you know that? Do any of you people know how hard he works? But Natalie and Susan and everybody else treat him like shit. Just like shit. No respect at all for his schedule. Do this, do that, and no warning whatsoever."

"So which'll it be, Mandy? I'm not trying to be an asshole here."

"But you're succeeding, so —"

"So I really need to see him and right now."

She jammed a finger against a button. Peter's disembodied voice said, "Yes?"

"Mr. Conrad is here." She made my name a thing that dripped with revulsion.

"Well, uh, bring him in." But he sounded

doubtful. He was obviously recalling our last meeting.

I'd never encountered this before, a district office that disliked — hell, despised — the congresswoman it represented. Apparently Peter and Mandy did their jobs well, tending to the various constituent services that the voters needed. And with an economy sinking lower every day, they had to be busier than ever. I wondered if they secretly drew mustaches on Susan's photographs after they closed up shop for the day.

"You can go in."

"Thank you, Mandy."

Her face wrinkled. She turned away. As I walked toward Peter's office, I saw the room where constituents filled out forms for help. The table sat twelve, six per side. All the seats were taken and half a dozen more people were standing around a coffeepot waiting for their turn to sit down. There would be a lot of heartbreak in that room.

Peter wore a gray suit, a white shirt, and a blue tie. With his sleek dark hair and bland smile he looked like every successful male senatorial staffer in Washington, D.C.

"I'll bet you're having a busy day," he said. He couldn't quite keep the sound of pleasure from his tone. He might be witnessing the downfall of his stepsister.

"Yep." I closed the door and walked over to one of the chairs in front of his desk. Photographs of major state pols from a generation ago, the men who would have helped him fulfill his dreams if only he'd had the guts and savvy to help himself. In the wide window behind him a 747 was just getting speed, elegant against the flat perfect blue of the sky.

"I'll do all I can."

"I'll bet."

"What's that supposed to mean?"

I'd been thinking about the newspaper story and all the inside information the reporter had gotten from somebody close to the campaign. What about a stepbrother who was jealous of his stepsister? "Somebody talked to that reporter. Somebody who knows the campaign. Otherwise that story would never have been written."

He'd been slouching. Now he sat up straight. He had Natalie's eyes. He could never match her scorn. He merely looked petulant.

He gritted his teeth and sighed. "Did Susan and Ben send you here to accuse me? They can shove this up their ass. I really resent this. I can't believe that my mother sanctioned this — you coming here."

"Things have moved way beyond what

your mother sanctioned or didn't sanction, Peter."

"This is total bullshit."

But everything — the body language, the anxiety in the gaze, the too-loud voice — told me he was lying.

I gave him my best lizard smile. "I talked to the reporter, Peter. I also offered him five hundred dollars to tell me who'd ratted out the campaign. He told me it was you." Lies can come in damned handy sometimes. He went back into his slump. He sulked. He waved a hand to dismiss me.

"I don't have to talk to you. I don't have to talk to anybody."

"Mommy's not going to be very happy when I tell her what you did. She's put an awful lot of money into this campaign," I said.

"You just get the hell out of here and don't ever come back."

"Mandy's going to stop me, is she? Between Mandy and Mommy, you're pretty well protected, aren't you, son?"

At the door I said, "You're a real piece of shit, you know that?"

Fortunately for both of us, Mandy wasn't in the reception area when I left.

CHAPTER 18

The press conference started promptly at three-twenty. Eighteen reporters filed into campaign headquarters and assembled in front of a rostrum we'd brought in. A good share of the office space used by the volunteers had been cleared to make more room for the press and a table had been set up with coffee and cookies. Staffers stood at the back, looking as if they'd been invaded and were just waiting for the jackboots to come back and kill them.

Susan arrived a few minutes after I did. I'd spent the earlier part of the afternoon working on our other two campaigns. Things were still going well for us, but there were problems my field people wanted me to work through with them. I spent half an hour in the gym. By the time of the press conference I'd cut my anxiety in half. I was stoned on some inexplicable form of optimism. Susan was not only going to do well, she was going to triumph.

In the staff office, she clutched my hand and said, "Wish me well."

I kissed her on the cheek. "You'll be fine, Susan. All you're going to do is tell the truth. You don't have anything to hide. That's all you need to remember. There's no reason to be on the defensive at all. And you've written a really fine statement to read."

She knew how to write and the words would be more meaningful if they were hers, rather than something contrived for her. I'd read them and they were good, strong, and honest. She'd dressed carefully, too. Her black pants suit was softened by a single strand of pearls. The burgundy blouse complemented her skin tone and the blonde chignon she had carefully fashioned. The look was efficient but still warm.

By the time we worked our way up front, the press was in place. There was the usual rumbling about deadlines and when the hell was this thing going to start, anyway. Ben and Kristin pacified them by pointing out that we were actually starting ten minutes earlier than we'd promised.

"Good afternoon," Susan said after stepping up to the microphone. By now there was a small bank of microphones from various TV and radio stations mounted on the rostrum. She'd always been comfortable with the press. "Thank you for coming here on such short notice. I know there is a story about me you'd like clarified, so I'll try to do that without keeping you too long. I know you're in a hurry to get your stories filed."

She glanced at me and then said, "And I'll take questions after my statement."

And so the beast set to feeding. Recorders were turned on, cameras focused, old-fashioned reporters' notebooks scribbled on as she began to read her statement.

"Twenty years ago I was a very different person than I am today. I was just out of college and living pretty selfishly. When I look back I'm not very fond of the young woman I was. One day I learned that I was pregnant. The man I was with wanted me to abort the child, and I have to admit that that was my first inclination, too. But something stopped me. I'd never really thought about abortion in a personal way. I was all in favor of a woman's right to choose — as I am today. But somehow it wasn't right for me. The father of my child and I went our separate ways. I had the child. But over the course of the next month I realized that I had too many personal problems to be a decent mother for my son. Maybe I was just being selfish; maybe I just didn't want the boy to interfere with my lifestyle. I took him to some nuns I knew at a convent near where I was staying. We talked for a long time, and the sisters decided that it would be best for the boy if they found a new home for him. It was a terrible experience for both my son and me. About a week after the nuns had taken him, I changed my mind in the middle of the night. I went to the convent. I was hysterical. I wanted my son back. But it was too late. Arrangements for a new family were under way. And I'm sure I didn't look very stable pounding on the convent doors at three in the morning. There hasn't been a day in my life when I haven't longed to know about my son. And there hasn't been a night when I don't wish I had kept him and raised him and let him know how much I loved him. And that's why I'm so happy to say that he's here in Aldyne and that we've been seeing each other and talking things through. My son's name is Bobby. He's married and I'm happy to say that his wife Gwen is pregnant. So not only am I a mom, I'm also about to become a grandmother. And I'm so grateful to the family that adopted him and gave him a good home."

I have to say that the press received all this respectfully. Yes, they gave her a respectful three or four seconds between the time she finished reading her statement and the time they started trying to rip apart what she said. They wanted to study the entrails for portents. But from the smiles Ben and Kristin were directing my way, I knew Susan had done very, very well.

Came the questions, came the answers: No, there was no point in naming the father. No, Bobby had not decided if he'd be staying in Aldyne. Yes, the friends of hers who mattered were happy for her. No, she didn't think this revelation would hurt her, and if it did she felt she had done the right thing, anyway — she was proud to acknowledge her son, she wasn't trying to hide it. No, there was no reason for Bobby to be interviewed right now — maybe later — but for now they were just getting to know each other. No, she didn't want to say anything more about Bobby at this time; if he wanted to come forward and talk to them, that would be his decision, not theirs. No, as she thought she'd made clear, she hadn't changed her mind on pro-choice — the decision she'd made twenty years ago was a personal one, not meant to make any kind of political statement.

All this took forty-three minutes. I kept shooting my cuff to keep track of the time. According to my watch, we had two minutes to go. That was the time we'd given the press. It was like sitting on a two-point lead in a basketball game. We needed to rush to the clock before any reporter lobbed a hand grenade.

Said hand grenade exploded with one minute to go. A pert young woman with horn-rimmed glasses and a stylish brunette bob had come in about ten minutes ago. I didn't know who she was or what station she was with. All I knew was that she had a camerawoman with her and that she was skillful at angling her way through the clutch of reporters. She hadn't asked a question until now, so Susan said, "Yes, Donna."

I had no idea who Donna was, but I was about to find out.

"The police are looking for a young man named Bobby Flaherty. They believe he has information about the murder of a man named Craig Donovan. Congresswoman Cooper, is Bobby Flaherty the son you've been talking about?"

This would be one for Donna's reel. TV reporters keep a tape of their best moments. They like to show a mix of the sentimental (kitten stories) and the bombastic (standing in front of a crooked businessman's door and demanding that he come out and answer some questions). This was a big moment for Donna's reel.

Susan's eyes went wide and wild — panic. She bumped into the podium. Ben started to lunge forward, then pulled himself back. He had to leave her alone. If he rescued her in some way, he'd only make things worse.

The expected rumble worked through the crowd. Donna's competitors would be pissed that she'd gotten the story before they did. A few of them were on their cells, calling their newsrooms for updates on the murder.

Susan took a deep breath, picked up her water glass, took a prim sip, set the glass down again, and said, "Yes, Bobby Flaherty is my son. I'm afraid I don't know what you're referring to, Donna. But I hope you and the others here will forgive me for leaving now. As Bobby's mother, I want to find out what's going on."

"Is there any possibility that he might be involved in this murder?" another reporter yelled.

Susan's gaze was hard now. "No chance whatsoever." And then she was turning away from the podium and they were shouting questions at her retreating form.

A handful of reporters tried to follow her back to the staff office, but Ben and Kristin and I moved fast enough to form a line that blocked them.

"Fun's over," Ben said. His voice was thin, as if he had trouble speaking.

Kristin glanced at me, shook her head. A camera caught her troubled expression and immortalized it. A telling image on the six o'clock news — Congresswoman Cooper staffer shocked at the breaking news about Bobby Flaherty.

"C'mon now," Ben said to the remaining reporters. We started herding them over to the door.

"You're Dev Conrad, right?"

"Yep."

The man asking the question aimed his microphone at me. "Did you get any warning about this?"

"We'll be issuing a statement very soon."

"Maybe the congresswoman doesn't know as much about her son as she thinks."

"We'll be issuing a statement very soon."

"Any chance she might withdraw?"

"Any chance I could get you to leave?"

"You getting tough?"

"No. You asked me a question. Then I asked you one."

"So you won't say anything on the record."

But we were at the door now. "I don't know about you, but I'm going to go have a very strong cup of coffee. I wish we had enough to go around, but I guess we're all out." Behind me I heard Ben laugh.

The reporter and his microphone finally left.

The volunteers had collected in a far corner. They resembled the stunned people you see immediately after tornados, intense distress that as yet they couldn't put into words. Hopes and dreams were collapsing, and they knew they were helpless to do anything about it.

Ben and I went back to the staff office. Kristin was alone there. She sat at her desk punching numbers into the phone with violent authority.

Ben and I listened.

Kristin spoke into the receiver: "Nick Rainey, please. This is Kristin Daly. Thank you." She cupped the phone and said to me: "The news director at Channel 4. He has a son-in-law who's a detective. His daughter is a big supporter of Susan's." Then: "Hi, Nick. I don't have to tell you why I'm calling. We just heard. I wondered if you could give me some background. All we got is that the police are looking for Bobby Flaherty to question him."

He spoke for a couple of minutes. All we heard was Kristin saying, "Yes" and "I see" and "Oh." Finally she said, "Thanks, Nick. I really appreciate this."

She turned her chair to face us. "Seems this Craig Donovan was sleeping with this local woman. She found him dead in his room. He'd been shot twice. The police think he was killed sometime last night."

"What the hell is going on?" Ben said. "This is crazy."

"Maybe not," I said. "Just stay focused on the money. Monica and Donovan were partners in blackmailing Susan. Wyatt delivers the money to Monica. Donovan wants it all for himself. He kills Monica."

"Then who killed Donovan?"

"Somebody who knew about the money and figured out that Donovan must have it. This person waits until Donovan is alone and then goes in, kills him, and takes the money."

"A quarter of a million dollars," Kristin said.

"Tax-free," Ben said.

"The stranglehold."

"What stranglehold, Dev?"

"Natalie's money. That's why Wyatt and

Manning, and even Susan to a degree, stay with her. They need her money. And she extracts her fee by humiliating and degrading them. But this time it was Donovan who had Natalie in the stranglehold. This time she got to know what it feels like."

"Don't try and make me feel sorry for Natalie," Kristin said. "I don't have that much empathy in me."

"I want to talk to Donovan's girlfriend," I said as I walked over and took my coat from the coat tree. "I'll stay in touch, but I probably won't be back for a while."

"I'll get a statement ready, and I'll read it to you over the phone for your changes."

"Thanks, Ben."

"I'm still thinking about Natalie being at somebody else's mercy. I'm a terrible person, I know, Dev. But I enjoy imagining how miserable she must be."

"I'm just as bad as you are, Kristin," I said, pulling on my coat. "The only good thing in all this is that maybe it'll teach Natalie a little humility."

When I got to the door, Kristin laughed and said, "Yeah, right."

The Stay-Rite hadn't changed, still the stucco-cracked, window-cracked hellhole it would always be. I wondered if Heather's

251

black eye had faded any.

I parked my rental in the nearest slot I could find. There were still several official vehicles taking up the other spaces and uniforms and forensic people combing the littered parking lot.

A battered SUV pulled in next to me, one of those despondent metal animals that would soon be laid to rest in a scrap yard. It had been red once, but now it was a pinkish color. And when the side door opened the hinges made a noise not unlike a scream.

Out stepped one of those ragged little women you always see in church basements where free food is given to the indigent. She wore a rumpled white Western hat, a Toby Keith T-shirt, and a pair of jeans that were ripped from age, not fashion. The sallow unhealthy skin and the desperate brown gaze made guessing her age impossible. She was likely a skinny, beaten forty going on seventy.

She had been facing me without looking at me. She went back to the SUV and reached in and withdrew a child of maybe three or four, a chubby but pretty kid. She took the little girl's hand, and they moved to the walk running in front of the motel.

The husband appeared then and he was a perfect match for his wife. The same unhealthy grayness of skin, the same forlorn look in the eyes. His T-shirt was from NASCAR. His Western hat was flat and black. And when he started to walk it was shocking and grotesque to see. He limped with such violence that most of his body was jerked about when he moved. The woman, still holding the little girl's hand, went over and slid her arm through her husband's. And it was the sort of thing that could break your goddamned heart because it was so simple and loving and said so much about their years together. They were playing a shitty hand, one the dark Love-craftian gods were probably still laughing about, but they were bound up and re-deemed by their loyalty.

The little girl smiled at me as they crossed in front of my windshield. I waved back. Then her mother saw me and smiled, too.

I didn't have any problem finding Detec-tive Kapoor. She appeared to be the only Indian woman in sight. She stood just inside the yellow crime-scene tape talking to a uniform. When she saw me she nodded in my direction. I doubted that she'd tell me much, but I waited her out.

The crowd was sparse. From what I'd been able to gather on the radio reports coming over here, the body had been discovered three hours ago. People had most likely drifted back to work. The crowd seemed to be residents here. A number of them stood in front of open motel doors. A baby bawled. A wind carried the scent of forensic chemicals from inside the murder room.

When Kapoor walked to the edge of the tape, she had her sleek head attached to a cell phone. She was laughing, but as soon as she clicked off the laugh died and she frowned at me.

I stood on my side of the tape.

"Unless you've come to answer my questions, I don't know why you're here, Mr. Conrad. You've been no help in the death of Monica Davies, and I'm sure you'll be no help with this one."

"You've already decided that Bobby Flaherty is guilty of this one, too."

She wore a dusky gray silk jacket and black skirt. The white blouse revealed small upscale breasts. "There is a connection between these two. As a citizen, I'd think you'd want to help us find out what that connection is."

"As I said, you've convicted him already."

"He's wanted for questioning." The dark eyes seemed amused now. "Just because he was seen at Monica Davies's room on the night of her murder and now we learn that he had several physical altercations with his father — why do you think I've convicted him already?"

I tried not to look surprised. I probably didn't pull it off.

A woman in a white lab coat appeared in the doorway of Donovan's room. "Detective Kapoor, would you come in here for a minute?"

"If you decide to be honest with me, Mr. Conrad, you can get hold of me day or night."

With that she was gone. In another situation I would have stayed to admire the elegant way she walked back to the room. For now, curiosity triumphed over idle lust. I needed to find Heather, the beautician who'd been staying with Donovan.

Hair Fare was located in a strip mall between a video shop and a pawn shop. One step inside I knew that this wasn't a place for men. Four women under hair dryers and four women in barber chairs gaped at me as if I were something rarely seen in this shop. The odors of the sprays and oils and lotions suffused my nostrils. I counted three Chicago Bears calendars and four Bears pennants.

The place was filled with posters and

counter displays for hair products. At a line of sinks against the back wall a woman was getting her hair washed. The beauticians wore their own clothes, no kind of uniforms at all. The last of them to look up from cutting hair was Heather. When she saw me her body jerked, as if she was going to bolt. "Sorry," said the older woman who was clearly Heather's sister. "We just cut for women here. Cost Cutters is just two blocks down."

"I'd like to see Heather when she's free. My name's Dev Conrad."

"Oh, yeah?" She was chewing gum. At the mention of Heather, she cracked it. She was heavier than Heather and not as pretty. She wore something that resembled a bouffant hairstyle and was dyed an orangish red. In her Bears sweatshirt and jeans she looked ready for a tailgater. She angled her head back to Heather and said, "You hear, this guy wants to see you."

"Well, I don't want to see him."

Sister smiled at me. The customers were intrigued by the potential for some nasty fun. "My sister's got a bad disposition."

"Really? I hardly noticed that."

A number of the customers laughed.

"I don't have to talk to you if I don't want to," Heather said.

Sister said, "She drop you, did she? You're better dressed than most of the bums she hangs out with. She should've hung on to you. She's always trying to find a rich one. You look like you might get lucky someday."

"I hope that's coming up soon."

She had an amazing female smile. "I didn't mean to give you a bad time. It's just that my little sister never stops getting into trouble."

"I don't want to talk to him and you can't make me."

"I think he's cute," said a woman in one of the barber's chairs. Three or four others laughed.

I was in a world of women and I didn't know the rules. Should I press the issue or just go away?

"I'm trying to help somebody who's in trouble, Heather. I need to talk to you."

"He's talking about the kid that killed Craig," Heather said from down the row, silver scissors poised to snip away at the garishly dyed red hair of her customer.

Sister said, "Didn't surprise me when somebody killed him. Man who hits women has got it coming. My sister's too dumb to understand that."

A woman in one of the chairs said, "I told my husband if he ever lays a hand on me

I'm gone for good and I'm taking the savings account with me."

"I wish I could convince my next-door neighbor of that," another woman said. "The son of a bitch she's married to is always hittin' her."

"You a friend of this kid Heather is talking about?" Sister asked.

"He's twenty. His wife is pregnant. He isn't really a kid."

"Heather likes 'em in their forties." Sister smiled. "That's why she thinks this guy is a kid." She glanced back at Heather again. "You get done with Shirley's hair there, you go in the back room and talk to this man."

"You don't have no right to boss me around like that."

"He's tryin' to help somebody, honey." There was an odd sweetness to her tone, as if she'd spent years hoping that her little sister would change her ways.

Sister pointed to a row of chairs lined across the front window. "There're some magazines there for you to read and you're welcome to help yourself to the coffee. She should be done in fifteen minutes or so."

"Thanks," I said, surprised at her largesse.

"All she can give you is a few minutes, though, Mr. Conrad. We're real busy today."

Heather scowled at me every thirty seconds or so as she cut her customer's hair. She seemed a lot more interested in me than her customer. This woman might end up with a very strange hairdo.

I tried reading an issue of *Cosmopolitan,* but I could only slog through a couple of the articles. Whatever happened to feminism? This was all man-pleasing stuff. I remembered reading my smart-ass uncle's magazines when I was in my teens. When he'd been in his teens, *National Lampoon* was at its height. They did a parody issue of *Cosmopolitan* and one of the articles was titled "Ten Ways to Decorate Your Uterine Wall." The magazine hadn't changed much.

"Mr. Conrad."

I'd switched to an elderly issue of *Time* and was engrossed in their predictions about the next election. Looked like Giuliani was a shoo-in for *el presidente.* I put the magazine down and looked up to see that Heather's customer was finished and walking toward the cash register. Sister was letting me know that Heather was ready for me. Or had damned well better be.

"This is really bullshit." As she spoke, Heather was sweeping up the floor around her chair. Sister ran a clean, tight shop. "The guy's a jerk." The ladies were getting a full measure of daytime drama right here in the beauty shop.

"You're the jerk," Sister said. "I told you not to get involved with that bastard."

By now I was getting used to the idea that the argument was public business. This whole salon was sort of like one big family. The other kids obviously sided with Sister.

"Thanks," I said as I walked past Sister toward a closed door in the back of the place. When I reached Heather's chair I stopped. She glared at me and shook her head. Then she gave up and flounced to the door, opened it, and disappeared inside.

It was a storeroom and office combined. There was a desk, a table for a computer and printer, a noisy refrigerator, and boxes piled floor to ceiling. Heather sat behind the desk and lit a cigarette. So much for the No Smoking law.

"This is really bullshit."

"You said that."

"That Bobby's an asshole. He came to the room three or four times. Craig always made me leave. I'd wait outside. I couldn't hear their words, but I could hear their voices. Bobby was always yelling. My opinion is that he snuck in and killed him. I want to see that little prick go to prison."

"And you told the police that?"

Exhaled ice-blue smoke. "Damn right,

that's what I told them."

"Did anybody else ever visit Donovan while you were there? That's what I'm trying to find out."

"I don't have to answer any of your questions."

"Didn't the police ask you the same question?"

"Yeah. So what?"

"What did you tell them?"

"I didn't tell them anything because it didn't matter. Bobby killed him and that's all there is to it."

"So somebody else came there, too?"

Another ice-blue stream of smoke. "Bobby killed him. Two nights me 'n' Craig were really getting along good, and then Bobby barges in and starts yelling and ruins the whole thing. Craig was in a shitty mood afterward. He gave me the black eye one of those nights. I blame Bobby for that. He had another fight with him the night before last."

A knock on the door. Sister peeked in. "Just wanted to see how it's going."

"He's tryin' to tell me that Bobby didn't kill Craig when I know damned well he did."

Sister said, "She being any help?"

"Not really. She wants to see Bobby get charged with the murder whether he did it

261

or not." Heather watched me with the fleshy face of a bellicose infant. "I'm pretty sure somebody else came to see Donovan while she was there, but she won't tell me who it was."

"That true, Heather?"

"How the hell would I know who came to see him? I wasn't there all the time."

Sister frowned. "I'm sorry, Mr. Conrad. She's got three more appointments back to back. Best I can do is give you a few more minutes." She closed the door. I listened to her walk back up front.

"He was gonna marry me."

"You really believe that?"

"Yeah, for your fucking information, I really did. He told me he'd come into a lot of money. A *lot* of money. He said he had these friends way down in Mexico, where the drug people would leave him alone. That's where he was gonna take me — until Bobby killed him."

Then she was up and charging around the side of the desk. She went right for the door. She had it open before I could stand up. "You heard my sister. We're real busy. Now, you quit botherin' me or I'm gonna call that detective, that colored one or whatever she is."

"She's Indian."

"Well, I'm gonna call her and tell her you're botherin' me. I'll bet she won't like that at all."

She walked out front. By the time I crossed the threshold, she was at her barber chair, feigning profound interest in her scissors.

I was on parade as I walked up to the cash register. As I passed Sister I said, "Thanks for trying to help."

"She's some piece of work, isn't she?"

A couple of the customers laughed.

As I opened the front door, two women whispered behind me. I didn't pick up on the words but I heard the giggles.

The motel had a central office and two wings that formed a V. After the Oklahoma City bombing we became aware of shadowy men who moved across the country staying in motels like this one, vague members of even vaguer groups that hated the government and hoped to destroy it. The feds began to miss the days when most of these people could be found in racist or seditionist compounds and were much easier to keep track of. Now they were scattered and impossible to track, much like the days before and during the Civil War when seditionists were hiding in the mazes of lodging houses in Washington, D.C., and other Northern cities.

Gwen had given me the room number. It was second from the end on the west half of the V. The newest car I could see was at least fifteen years old. A baby cried in one room, in another a TV preacher shouted Bible words, and in a third a woman wept. I knocked on Gwen's door. She opened it immediately.

She wore another faded maternity top. This one was a kind of puce color. She'd put on makeup and combed her hair. The gamine face was somber. "He isn't here, Mr. Conrad."

I'd hoped to get something helpful from Heather before coming out here. Something that would help make my case when I talked to Bobby — but nothing.

"You know the police are looking for him. And there isn't any time for this, Gwen. He's in real trouble. Now let me in."

"I told you, Mr. Conrad, he isn't —"

"Gwen, listen. He's inside and he's in trouble. I'm trying to put this whole thing together. He can help me and maybe I can help him."

"Oh, Mr. Conrad . . ."

"Screw it, let him come in." A male voice, young, despondent.

"You sure, honey?"

"Am I sure? Of course I'm not sure. I'm not sure of a thing right now. But you might as well let him in." Hard to know which was the dominant tone, the fear or the self-pity.

"He didn't kill anybody, Mr. Conrad. He really didn't."

I followed her into a room that was a coffin of old griefs and old fears, the sort of place the human animal goes to hide out like any other animal that is being chased by yesterday. The room was painted mustard yellow. There was a double bed that appeared to slant from both ends into the middle. The ugly brown bedspread once had merry nubs on it. Most of the nubs were gone. There was a bathroom. The doorknob was missing, so all that remained was a hole. The tiles on the room floor curled upward in places. I couldn't be sure, but tiny pieces on the floor looked like rat droppings.

Bobby Flaherty sat in the only chair, a beaten armchair with so many stains they looked like part of the design. He was a handsome kid in a sullen way. He wore a black sweatshirt, jeans, and blue running shoes. Gwen closed the door behind me. "You be nice to him, Bobby. He wants to help us."

Bobby added to the haze of smoke in the

room by tamping out another cigarette from the pack on his lap. He dug out a long blue plastic lighter and snicked it into flame. He blew out enough smoke to hide behind. He just watched me, animal-alert, assessing a potential enemy.

"You call the police before you came over here?"

"No. I wanted to talk to you."

"You be nice," Gwen snapped. She might have been talking to her snarling dog. "Tell him you appreciate how he's helped me. You promised you would."

He laughed but in a tender way. "Honey, I do appreciate it. But I want to make sure he didn't call the cops. Is that all right?"

"He said he didn't call the police. And I believe him."

He stared at me through the blue haze. "All right, I believe him." Then: "I didn't kill anybody."

"All right. But you were seen running from Monica Davies's room. And there's a witness who said you've had several fist-fights with your father."

"Heather," he said. "He could really pick 'em."

The east wall hummed with TV dialogue from the room next door. I sat on the edge of the bed.

"How did your father get back in touch with you?"

"Why?"

"Because your mother is very worried about you. And so is Jim Shapiro and so am I. You've got to face this, Bobby. I'm trying real hard to believe you're innocent, but I have to know what happened, starting with your father coming back into your life."

"If you don't tell him, Bobby, I will. You need to let him help us."

Bobby's glance met hers. He sighed and looked back at me. "I got adopted out to the Flahertys when I was little, that's where I picked up the name. I didn't know anything about my old man until a year ago. He managed to track me down." The smile was bitter. "He was a con man. Did some time in Joliet for running a scam in Chicago, so he wouldn't have had much trouble getting through the adoption system and finding out where I lived. He gave them a bullshit story that they went for. He was very good at bullshit." There was nothing but contempt in his voice for his father. "But I'm probably being hypocritical. I did a little time in county myself. The six longest months of my life. Got drunk and got into a fight and beat the guy up pretty bad. By then the Flahertys didn't want me around anymore and I couldn't blame them. I'd been in trouble a lot in school and they just couldn't deal with me anymore. All the time I was in county I kept thinking of how good they'd been to me and how I'd hurt them. I was a real asshole."

"But you're not anymore, honey."

This smile was warm. "She's my number-one fan."

"What did your father say to you when he found you?"

He fired up another cigarette. As a card-carrying liberal I should have whipped out my CD about the dangers of secondhand smoke, especially around pregnant women, but I decided I'd be selfish and push him for more information instead.

"He gave me a line of crap about how sorry he was he'd never contacted me and how he wanted to make it all up to me and how he'd had some rough times — the way he told it, he was just in the wrong place at the wrong time and he'd made the mistake of hanging around the wrong kind of people and he'd had a bad childhood, all the usual bullshit — and that he wanted to help me make some money so I could get the chance in life that he'd never had. I just sort of watched him — I actually thought it was kind of funny. The way he was trying to work me, I mean. I think he actually thought I believed everything he was saying about wanting to be my old man now and how we'd hang together the rest of our lives."

"He scared me. There was just something about him." Gwen had her hands pressed protectively against her stomach as she said this. "And I hated what he got Bobby involved in."

Bobby's shrug hinted at my reaction to her words. Bobby was smart. Bobby was tough. Nobody involved him in anything — he involved himself.

"The blackmail?"

"Yeah."

"His idea was to present you as proof that you were his son with Susan Cooper?"

"Right. We were going to make a lot of money. And the way he figured it, we'd keep on making money as long as she kept running for office."

"I was totally against it," Gwen said. "By that time I hated that man. And now look what's happened."

"Why did you go to Monica's room?"

His eyes found his wife's. "I was going to tell her to forget it. That I didn't want any part of what she and my old man were up to. I wasn't getting anywhere with my old man, so I thought I'd try Monica. Gwen really leaned on me about it. She said that she didn't want to bring our baby into the world this way. When I got there Monica was already dead. I ran and that's when somebody saw me. And as soon as Mr. Shapiro got me out of jail, I went to my old man's to tell him the same thing — that I didn't want my name mixed up in it, that I was going to have a kid now. He didn't care."

"How did Larson get involved in this? He said that Monica worked this by herself."

"I don't know. He just started showing up and one day we got into it. All I knew was that the money was coming from Natalie. And Monica was handling that. Larson wanted to know all the details."

"Bobby, do you have any idea who killed Donovan and Monica?"

He ran a rough hand across his face. "No. When that Indian detective was firing questions at me, I kept wishing that I knew a name to give her. But I don't."

"You need to turn yourself in, Bobby."

He glared at Gwen. "I told you that he'd say this." His gaze on me was no less harsh. "No way, man. We can raise our baby in Mexico. Start a life there."

"You read much about Mexico lately, Bobby?"

"You mean all the drug gangs? I know how to handle myself. And I know how to stay out of trouble."

At any other time I would have smiled. The life he'd described as his own had been nothing but trouble, ending in this motel room wanted for two murders.

Gwen said, "I don't want to move to Mexico. But I don't want Bobby to give himself up, either. I might never see him again." She put her head down and started crying softly. Bobby got up and went over and sat next to her on the bed. He held her and I felt good for both of them. He was troubled and half crazed, but he knew enough to care for the one person in his life whose love was clean and true.

I made an effort to sound gentle. "You can't run, Bobby. There's no place to go. And I doubt you have any money."

Gwen sobbed, "You can't expect him to turn himself in!"

"Shapiro's a good lawyer. Running will just make things worse."

"I won't let him turn himself in! I'll never see him again!" Gwen sobbed even louder.

"There's no other choice right now, none."

But Bobby's expression had softened. His gaze was more sorrowful than belligerent. He took her to him and held her close and kissed the top of her head. I hoped that my daughter's someday man would be this loving. Then he started slowly shaking his head, staring at the wall. He must have realized that I was right. Mexico was a pipe dream. And where would he go if he stayed in the States?

I had my own realization to face. There was no way any of this would stay out of the press for long. Police departments are filled with snitches eager to call reporters. And given Susan's liberal record, they'd likely be eager to help Duffy. Not all of them, but most of them. I hoped that when the news broke, Duffy would be sensible enough to go out and get drunk for at least a day. I would. As for our campaign, we'd be playing defense right up until the election. If neither Susan nor Natalie had anything to do with the murders, the scandal would settle on her bearing a child she'd put up for adoption in her wild days. In recent years some people had been reelected after being outed as wife beaters, check forgers, hooker lovers. The only thing in our favor was that this was an old story. And being cynical, if we could put Susan and Bobby in a loving interview together, maybe we could get lucky and find sentiment on our side.

Bobby said, "Call Mr. Shapiro, I guess."

"No!" Gwen cried. She was coming apart and I felt like hell for being a part of it. Then she lay back on the bed and covered her face with her hands.

I slid my cell phone out of my pocket. Bobby held Gwen even tighter. Then she was struggling up and heading to the bathroom. Moments later she began to vomit.

CHAPTER 19

When the police station came into view, Bobby made a grunting sound as if he'd been punched in the belly. "This might be the last day I ever spend outside of jail. Maybe Gwennie's right."

"I don't believe that." The day had turned cold and windy; the light rental rocked as wind gripped it. We had stashed Gwen in a nice warm hotel room.

"Yeah? And what's that supposed to mean to me? You're in this because of some stupid political campaign. I'm in this for my life."

I pulled into the parking lot and shut down the motor. I sat there silent for a long moment, then said, "Bobby, I'll tell you what. You think I don't want to help you and Gwen, how about this? You open that door and start running. I'll give you two hours before I let the police know about any of this. How's that sound?"

He fell back against the seat. He was still

strapped in. His eyes closed. From what I could tell, a sob had caught in his throat. "I should never have listened to my old man. I suppose I did because I'm just like him."

"No, you're not. That's bullshit and you know it. The way you treat Gwen, the way you love her — from what I know of your old man, that wasn't him at all. And you backed out. You told him that and you went to see Monica to tell her that." I hesitated to say this because I wasn't sure it was true. "You take after your mother."

He didn't speak for a time. He brought his head up and stared out the side window. A few cars passed, their exhaust silver ghosts in the daylight. A black-and-white squad car pulled into the lot and went on past us to the back of the station where a number of other black-and-whites were parked. Wind came then and grasped the rental from below and rocked it back and forth like a boat. In the glass, Bobby was wiping his tears with his fingers and taking deep breaths. "You trust that detective?" He was back to looking at me again.

"Kapoor? Yeah. For a cop, I mean. She's got her job to do and we've got ours. She'll try and nail you and we'll try to show her that she's wrong. Jim Shapiro knows what he's doing."

"I get the feeling you do, too."

"Well, maybe. I hope so. If this thing isn't going our way by tomorrow afternoon, I'm sending for a private detective we work with in Chicago. He's relentless."

A second black-and-white swept in and headed for the rear of the building.

"I really want to open this door and just start running."

"I know you do."

"And you wouldn't stop me?"

"No."

"Poor Gwennie."

"Think of what you running would do to her, Bobby. She doesn't want to think of you in jail, but think of the nightmares she'd have if you were on the run. Not knowing where you were, how you were surviving. Always worried that you'd draw a bad cop some night and he'd kill you just for sport. Think of that, Bobby. Think of what it'd do to your wife and what it'd do to your baby."

He opened the door and angled around in the seat as if he were going to get out. Then he just sat there. The wind rocked the car again. The cold chased all the heat out of the rental.

He got out then and just stood there, gaping around as if he'd awakened in a new realm. Then he ducked his head back in and said, "C'mon. We might as well get this bullshit over with." Then: "Think you could pick me up a couple packs of smokes and drop them off? I've only got about five or six left in this pack. Generics'd be fine."

"What kind do you like when you can afford them?"

"Regular Winstons, I guess."

"I'll get you a couple of those."

He nodded and withdrew his head.

A quick minute later we were walking through the front doors of the police station.

It was the day of weeping women.

We passed three young black men watching us suspiciously just inside the doors as we walked up to the information counter. Behind us we heard sobbing. In the corner where I'd waited this morning a young black woman was trying to comfort a sobbing middle-aged woman I guessed was her mother. They both wore Bears jackets and jeans. Large cheap purses squatted on the floor next to them like waiting pets. Her sobs were so sharp I felt them physically. Helpless proximity to suffering is a form of suffering itself.

"May I help you?" This was a female cop in a light-blue uniform shirt. She was built like a wrestler and had a voice to match.

"I'd like to talk to a detective. Preferably Detective Kapoor."

"What's this about, sir?"

"I'd rather discuss that with the detective."

"Well, Kapoor — she's in court right now."

"Well, then, whatever detective's on duty, I guess."

"And your name?"

"Dev Conrad."

"And yours?" Her eyes met Bobby's.

He mumbled, "Bobby Flaherty."

The hard blue eyes bloomed with recognition. "You go sit down over there. I'll have a detective out here right away."

We went to the waiting area and sat down. The older woman had quit crying and had now folded her hands in her lap. Her lips told me she was making a silent prayer. She was worn beyond her years, sweat sheening her dark skin. It wasn't hot in here. The sweat came from panic and terror. I'd caught just enough of her conversation to recognize that one of her children was in one of the interrogation rooms and that he was in the kind of trouble that would send him away for long years that only his mother would worry about.

Bobby closed his eyes and set his head

against the wall. His sighs came out as daggers. His jaw muscles were busy and his shoes danced in time to music only he could hear.

The detective who appeared resembled the broker my firm used. I put his age at late thirties. He wore a good blue suit, a quiet blue-on-blue tie, his thinning hair was cut military-school short, and he proffered a smile that said he was happy to meet us, even though "us" included a young man who just might have popped two people.

"My name's Detective Brian Courtney. Why don't we take a walk down the hall over here and I'll hunt up some coffee for us."

The officer at the information desk watched Bobby with her upper lip curled up. She was probably around fifty and hadn't yet acclimated herself to the public-relations approach cops took these days, at least when there were witnesses around.

Courtney put us in a small beige room with five folding chairs and a five-foot-long folding table. We were being videotaped — standard operating procedure. "I'll get us that coffee."

Courtney came back with three paper cups of vending-machine coffee. He did this while opening and closing the doors. When he set them down, he said, "It tastes like shit, but hey, it's warm, right?" Then he did Police 101. "Bobby, let's get the basic facts down fast, and then we can go back for the details."

"What facts?" Bobby snapped.

"Basically, how you killed them — the Davies woman and your father."

Bobby lurched from his chair. I was sitting next to him and grabbed his arm and forced him to sit back down.

"We didn't come here to confess," I said. "Bobby didn't have anything to do with those murders. There's a warrant out for his arrest. All we're doing is honoring the warrant. And in a few minutes Jim Shapiro will be here, and I don't plan to say anything else about the case until he's here."

"Jim Shapiro. Must be nice to have the kind of money it takes to hire him."

"He says it's pro bono. He believes, as do I, that Bobby didn't have anything to do with the crimes."

"Pro bono. Jim must have bought his allotment of classic MGs for this year. He collects them, you know."

"Yeah, I heard they were going to pass a law against that. It must've gotten through, huh?"

It was at that moment that he discovered

me. I'd just been some nuisance bastard dragging a double-murderer into his clutches, but now I was as much his enemy as Bobby was. Now I was real and he didn't like me at all.

"Exactly what is your interest in this?" His fake cordiality had a nasty edge to it now.

"I'm a friend of his wife's."

"Oh? And how does that work?"

"It 'works' that I'm a friend of his wife's."

"Uh-huh. Are you a lawyer, Mr. Conrad?"

"No, I'm not. I'm a political consultant."

You could see all the computing going on behind the robot eyes. "I see. And you're working in this area?"

"My firm is. For the Cooper campaign."

The smile was deadly. "Congresswoman Cooper. I wouldn't advertise that in this building if I was you."

A knock interrupted our sparring. A voice said: "I've got Jim Shapiro out here, Lieutenant. All right if he comes in?"

"Fine. Send him in."

Shapiro came in like a bullet. He looked ready for court in a custom-cut gray pin-striped suit. He carried a briefcase and a cup of 7-Eleven coffee. He smelled of masculine cologne and cold air. He set the briefcase on the table and nodded to me. He didn't look at Bobby; instead his eyes focused on Courtney. "You're not nearly as pretty as Kapoor, Brian."

"Kapoor is in court. I got ahold of her. She's on her way. For now here I am and here you are and now that you're here I don't know exactly why our friend Mr. Conrad has to sit in."

Shapiro's tone was icy. "He did you and the police force a big favor, Lieutenant. This was successfully resolved without anybody being injured." The implication being that Courtney might be disappointed about that fact.

Courtney shrugged. "Whatever. I'd be just as happy if he left."

I was on my feet before Jim Shapiro could say anything. Bobby watched me with the eyes of a child who knew he was about to be deserted.

"It's been a pleasure, Lieutenant."

"Right back at you, Mr. Conrad."

Shapiro glanced at me, then at Courtney, then back at me. He laughed. "I take it you two aren't in danger of falling in love, huh?"

"He works with Congresswoman Cooper."

"Oh, yes, the dreaded Congresswoman Cooper. Hell, Brian, I'm one of her supporters, too."

"Right. But Mr. Conrad here is actually in the business of getting her elected."

282

"Thanks, Jim." I reached over and put my hand on Bobby's shoulder. His eyes were despondent; his mouth was crimped. "Jim'll call me when this is over, Bobby. We're going to take care of this. I promise you."

I knew I was amusing Courtney. He was taking great pleasure in my frustration.

Shapiro patted me on the back. I went to the door. I thought of looking back, taking a last shot at Courtney. But what would be the point?

I opened the door and stepped into the hall. A friendly face above a blue uniform said, "There's some fresh coffee in the break room down the hall. You won't have to drink any more of that machine crap."

"Thanks," I said. I had a fair share of police friends in Chicago. Nice to know that the Aldyne police had at least one member who decided that civility wasn't an admission of weakness.

But all I wanted was to get out of the station house. My footsteps snapped down the polished floor of the corridor and around a corner. Detective Kapoor, sheathed in a sleek blue suit, had probably been checking something at the front desk before heading to the interrogation room.

When she saw me, her dark eyes gleamed with humor. "Good to see you again, Mr.

Conrad."

"I just met your Detective Courtney."

The smile now touched her rich red lips. "Careful what you say. He hears every-thing."

"That doesn't surprise me. The problem is he's hearing things that aren't true. Bobby Flaherty didn't kill anybody."

"And you're going to do our department the favor of telling us who did?"

"Maybe even better. How about you tell me since you're the police and I'm not?"

The polite smile left the perfectly con-structed face. "Detective Courtney and I have put together a good preliminary case against your young friend, Mr. Conrad. That doesn't mean we'll stop looking for other suspects. But it does mean that we've got good sound reasons to make him our chief suspect, at least for the time being."

She started walking past me before I could say anything. "Have a good day, Mr. Con-rad." Not favoring me with a look back as she spoke.

Then I was outside in a lashing wind and hurrying to my rental.

CHAPTER 20

Sitting in a Starbucks, I used my cell phone to call Heather at her sister's beauty shop. Sister answered the phone, and when I identified myself, she said, "I've been working on her but she won't tell me anything. She got drunk last night and didn't come in until late this morning. She's not in real good shape. I'll do my best to get her to talk to you."

"I appreciate that. Thanks."

I called the office and spoke to Ben.

"I got a call from a media rep, Dev. He said Duffy's media man just made a big buy for both thirty-second and ten-second spots. And he's heard that he's buying them all over the district."

"They're going to jump on it. But Duffy's smart. He won't come at us head-on. It'll all be by inference."

"The rep says he'll let me know the minute they get a spot. I'll run out there to look at it."

"I can see it now. Three women sitting at a table and an off-camera voice says, 'Will the woman who had a child out of wedlock please raise her hand?' And then the Susan look-alike will not only raise her hand, she'll start bawling her ass off because she's so ashamed of herself."

"You should be in advertising."

"Please, isn't politics scummy enough for you?"

He laughed. "Good point."

"Keep me posted."

"Sure thing."

Over coffee and a muffin I tried to make it as simple as possible. Craig Donovan and Monica Davies blackmailed Natalie. Natalie paid them the money. Monica was killed in her hotel room. I was assuming that Donovan had killed her and taken the money for himself because there was a good chance that his murder had also been a robbery. The longer I thought about it, Susan's words played into my take on everything. "He's the most devious person I've ever known — a sociopath who loves to play games. He'd blackmail people, and then when they paid him, he'd immediately demand more. Right on the spot. He told me he knew he couldn't get it; he just liked

286

to see them suffer. He enjoys the torture as much as the money." But in this case maybe he didn't just want to see Natalie suffer; he wanted more money for real. But now it was moot. Alive, he could have talked to the press and revealed a lot of Susan's secrets from her days of drinking and drugging. That would have been his last resort. But he was dead and so were all his secrets. Now the problem was finding the killer. Our last chance at recovering from the Bobby story was getting ahead of the next one. The police were happy to keep Bobby in jail, case closed.

I decided to drive to the foundation. I hadn't talked to David Manning yet. He might have connections with the press that even we didn't. He was a local, and as head of a nonprofit, he'd know local important people. Management and CEO-level people who just might have a hand in controlling local media. Getting even one sympathetic outlet for our story would help. Fog and drizzle gave the afternoon streets a water-color patina. Stoplights burned through the clouds like spreading wounds. I found an oldies station. Music transports me back into the past faster than anything else. I was once again a teenager of no particular note, given to a brown leather bomber jacket that was obstinate proof of my coolness. There's a lot of self-pity in looking back — you want to look at who you were and warn him, make him smarter and tougher. You want to protect him. He is almost your child. Then I thought of Susan as a teenager. I wondered if she'd worn one of those bombastic hairstyles you saw on music videos. Then I thought of Jane, tried to picture her. Somehow the mental photo had her in jeans and a T-shirt, and smiling the way she had at dinner. The image made me smile.

And then I thought of Craig Donovan — no specific image, just a feeling of anger and dread. The most difficult thing for most people to imagine is evil. Real evil. Not Hollywood evil. The obvious ones are the drifters and the hobos and the lonely little ones who are invariably described as "quiet" when they're caught after killing six or seven women. But then there are the swaggerers. They have looks and sometimes charm. I kept thinking about how he tortured his blackmail victims. I kept thinking about how many people he'd likely killed before, during, and after the time Susan had traveled with him. But at some point his luck had run out. The clothes weren't so good, the motel was a shithole, and he'd put on the kind of weight that gave him a thuggish look. The man I'd fought with the other night was a career criminal destined to live out his days in a maximum-security prison. He'd had his vengeance for Susan deserting him, though. He'd forced her to publicly face her past.

The Cooper Foundation stood stout and stern against the dim day, the classic red brick with its concrete parapet and wide front steps, impenetrable by any agent except time itself. The lot on the east side of it was only half full, so I had no trouble finding a spot. I hurried through the drizzle and walked inside. The museum setting of the first floor imposed quiet the way a church does. I'd seen this floor in brochures. The walls told their stories in paintings, photographs, and the drawings of children — expressions of suffering from every part of the planet. Senator Cooper's wife had wanted everybody to understand that while they were enjoying happy hour a good share of the world was dying of famine and illness and war. These were the places the Cooper Foundation sent its money. I remembered Ben making a joke about how different the foundation would have been if the second Mrs. Cooper — Natalie — had set it up. "It'd all go to fashion designers and Paris

Hilton types. You know, the *real* Americans."

I crossed the parquet floor to the front desk — the solemn air filled with Debussy on the sound system — where a young black woman sat reading a book. She smiled when she looked up. She was quite pretty, winsome, in her crisp white blouse. There was a hint of mischief in her eyes as she saw me trying to read the title on the spine of her paperback. *"Sister Carrie,"* she said. "Theodore Dreiser."

"One of my favorite novels."

"Really?"

"Sure. Mandatory reading for people my age who grew up in Chicago." *Sister Carrie* was about a country girl who comes to Chicago at the turn of the last century and uses her looks and cunning to become a creature of high society. It is a brilliant, bitter novel.

"God, the story's fascinating, and the way Chicago was back then . . ." She had a wonderful smile. "My English professor said it was banned in places when it first came out."

"The publisher said he was sorry it was ever brought out."

She had a sweet smile and a smart laugh. "It always amazes me what was so scandalous back then. She'd be on a reality show today." She put her slender hand forth. "I'm Keisha, by the way. I work here after my college classes are over, answer the phone and greet people and do homework when nothing's going on."

"Dev Conrad. Is David Manning in, do you know?"

"No. They've been trying to find him. When I come in I always check upstairs with Doris. She's very upset. Scared, I think. Nobody's heard from him all day."

"Doris is in then?"

"Yes. Would you like to see her?"

"Please."

Nobody's heard from him all day, I thought as she picked up her phone and punched in a single digit. "Hi, Doris, it's Keisha. There's a Mr. Conrad to see you. Is it all right if I send him up?" Pause. "Thanks, Doris." Then: "You can go right on up. She sits at the reception desk. The other offices and the conference room are behind her. If you need to see anybody else, she can direct you."

"Enjoy the book, Keisha."

"Oh, I am. I just can't help feeling sorry for Carrie sometimes — I don't think I'm supposed to feel that, do you?"

Before I could answer, her phone rang and she started explaining to someone how a group went about setting up a tour for an entire class. She gave me a little wave.

The upstairs was all business. Wine-red carpet instead of parquet flooring, the walls covered with photographs of the late senator and various dignitaries of various eras, and a front desk wide enough to play tennis on. Doris Kelly looked almost childlike sitting at it. There was no music up here. She didn't seem to hear me until I stood right in front of her desk. When she looked up, I saw her pull open a drawer and drop something inside quickly. She closed it with a look of shame. "I really shouldn't be doing that, Mr. Conrad." She knew I'd glimpsed what she'd hidden away. "I'm not a very good Catholic. I only go to Mass occasionally, but, of course, whenever something bad happens, there's old hypocrite Doris saying her rosary."

Tears had stained the flower-blue eyes red. The nostrils were red, too. A small box of Kleenex sat next to her phone setup. Today's suit was black — I wondered if she believed in omens — the blouse fuchsia.

"All I got was from Keisha downstairs."

"She's such a sweetheart." She plucked a tissue from the box and dabbed her eyes and nose. "We've been calling everywhere all day. He had a meeting at a bank and a meeting with an investment group. He spends a lot of time talking to financial people, trying to steer some of their wealthiest clients to put us on their list of charities. He's very good at it."

"When was the last time anybody here talked to him?"

"From what I can tell, it was Keisha. She said she worked until five forty-five and walked out with him. She said he locked up and said good night and then walked to the lot and got in his car. I'd usually have been here, but I had a four o'clock appointment with my doctor. You know how doctors' offices are. I didn't get in until nearly five. Oh, God, I'm just babbling, aren't I?" Her voice was trembling.

"You've called Ben?"

"Yes. I didn't tell him what was going on. I didn't want to alarm him. Or anybody there. But I said we really needed to hear from David in case he made contact with campaign headquarters."

"Has David ever done anything like this before?"

She looked at me as if I'd asked a dirty question. "Of course not. He's the most responsible man I've ever known."

She was talking about the man she loved, that was obvious. Whether David felt the same way, I had no idea.

"I was thinking of calling the police."

"No!" My anger surprised me. "Sorry. I didn't mean to snap there. But no — we've got enough problems with the press, and if we bring the police in on this the press will have another story to flog us with."

"I happen to care about him very much." She blushed.

"Look, Doris. We don't know what's going on. People just walk away from things sometimes. Not for long. They just take a day off. I've done it myself. Haven't you?"

"I have a perfect employment record. You never know when you might need your employer to give you a recommendation."

She was starting to irritate me. It was easy to see her now as the snitch in grade school who reported everything to the teacher.

"The police wouldn't do anything, anyway. There'd be no reason to. Not at this point. Did you try his home?"

"Yes. I talked to the maid. She said that David came home late and went to bed. She said he had an early breakfast and left for the office. That was around seven o'clock. Nobody's seen or talked to him since." She touched a slender finger to the Kleenex box; there seemed to be solace in the act because she sighed. "I'm just so worried about him."

I took out my card and placed it on her desk. "There's my cell phone. No matter what time it is, if you learn anything, call me. Meanwhile, I'll do some checking of my own."

"You'll really help me with this?"

"Of course. I just want to keep it quiet while I'm doing it."

"I'm sorry, Mr. Conrad. This has — this has just really frightened me."

She'd always called me Mr. Conrad, even when the group of us had had dinner in Chicago. She was just being proper, I supposed, the way her favorite book instructed her to — *The Secretary's Guide to Anal-Retentive Behavior.* There was no point now in trying to get her to call me Dev.

"Remember, call me the minute you hear anything."

"I will. Of course I will."

I reached over and placed my hand on hers. "This'll have a happy ending, Doris. He'll turn up and he'll be fine. You'll see."

Then I was walking to the stairs. I wondered how long it'd be before she hauled her rosary out again.

On the way to campaign headquarters I punched between three radio call-in shows. Each was dealing with the subject of Congresswoman Cooper's son and the fact that he was being held for questioning by police. Somewhere amid the din of disapproval there was a gentler, more reasoned voice, female, making the point that a fair number of women had put illegitimate children up for adoption and that the fact that they were together again would be good for both of them. And that maybe we — the public we — should wait to see what kind of evidence the police had before judging Bobby guilty. She wasn't on long. Who wanted to hear this kind of conciliatory crap when finding a tree for lynching was so much more fun?

At four-thirty in the afternoon the front of headquarters was empty except for volunteer staffers. Between rain, fog, and headlines the usual crew of young helpers had found other things to do after school. In the staff office in back, only Ben and Kristin remained. Kristin was laboring through a telephone conversation with a reporter who was obviously checking out various rumors. Duffy was probably floating a few of them — just as we would — but this kind of situation produces fictions through some kind of organic process that borders on magic. *Then Susan wasn't a lesbian after all? Had Susan produced other illegitimate children we didn't know about and were any of them of the colored persuasion perhaps? Was there any possibility that Susan had been impregnated by an alien and that Bobby was a Venusian spy?*

I got myself a cup of coffee and sat down at a Mac to check my e-mail. I needed to get caught up on the two other races my company was handling. The news made me feel better than it should have. I was probably just thankful that there weren't any scandals associated with either one. We were holding small leads in both, but right now that felt like smashing victories.

"I'm meeting somebody for an early dinner," Kristin said, slipping into her tan Burberry and grabbing her umbrella. "If either of you need me, I'll keep my cell on."

"What could go wrong?" Ben said. "Not on this campaign."

Kristin laughed. "Oh, God, don't even joke about it. I just keep thinking the worst is over and then something else happens. It's been like that since they found Monica Davies in her hotel room."

"Dev here has assured me that if we can just keep Susan's police record as a hooker away from the press, everything'll be fine."

"And don't forget when she was teaching grade school and selling crack to her students," I said. I was glad to be making fun of it all. At this point there wasn't much else to do with it. "But I'm pretty sure that won't come out, either."

"You two are terrible," Kristin said. "You should have more respect for teachers who sell crack to their third-grade students."

And with that she was gone into the cold, wet, black afternoon.

Ben took three calls from the press with no more than a few minutes between each one. He was patient and professional until the very end of the third one, when his sighs filled the room. "No, I told you Bobby hadn't been officially charged with murder. Right now all they're doing is questioning him." Pause. "I know there's a story on one of the radio stations that he's been charged, but it isn't true and that's why we don't have a statement about him being charged." Pause. "I'll tell you what, Nina. Call the police station. They'll confirm what I've said." Pause. "You're welcome."

After he hung up, he turned in his chair and said to me, "Kristin's off to meet the new one."

"I figured."

"It won't work out any better than the other ones, but right now she won't admit that to herself."

"But as soon as he mentions settling down

and raising a family —"

"Kristin's a political junkie just like us. She should settle down and have kids, but she probably won't."

"Look at her role models — you and I were shit parents. No offense."

"She'd be a hell of a lot better at it than we were."

"That wouldn't be too hard."

I always wondered if that wasn't one of the reasons Ben and I were such good friends. We'd only gotten to know our children after they were grown. There was a lot of remorse and shame in our conversations.

But now it was back to work. We both knew what we were up against, and that the odds of succeeding were getting longer by the hour. I'd spent half a delusional day convincing myself that after a fess-up press conference the story would go away. But we'd had to play defense at the press conference. And we hadn't expected the news about Bobby being sought by the police.

Another reporter called. Ben went back at it. He threw fastballs, sliders, curves. Ben at his best, which was very, very good.

And while he was talking I wrote e-mails to the managers of our other two campaigns. One of them wrote back immediately, saying that the Susan story was starting to get traction up where he was working. Not what I wanted to hear.

I was thinking about dinner and a few drinks when the cell phone in my pants pocket bleated. I didn't recognize the number of the caller. "Hello."

"Mr. Conrad?" The voice was unmistakable. Sister from the beauty shop.

"Yes."

She identified herself and then said, speaking quietly, almost a whisper, "We'll be closing up here pretty soon. I had a talk with Heather and I'm real worried about her. She says she's gonna leave town tonight."

"Did she say why?" I tried not to sound excited — you know, like a doctor when he sees a thirty-pound tumor; nothing here to get agitated about at all, Mr. Gleason — so I stayed calm. But obviously Heather was afraid now and I wondered why.

"She —" Now her words were barely audible. "Could you just come over here? I need to go. She's coming back here to the office now." She clicked off.

Ben was answering another call as I hung up. I heard him say, "Yes, Natalie. He's right here."

Ben waggled the receiver in my direction and rolled his eyes. Sotto voce he said,

"She's pissed off!"

I punched in the blinking line and picked up the receiver. "Hi, Natalie."

"This is to inform you that as of this moment our reelection campaign is officially being run by Crane and Wilbur from Washington, D.C. In return for your help with any transition problems they might have, I'll personally see to it that all your reasonable fees and charges are paid promptly."

I was pretty sure she'd written this down and was reading it.

"They're flying six people out here tomorrow morning. I'll be announcing the changeover tonight. I've called two newspapers and three TV stations. I plan to be professional. All I'll say is that we had certain intractable disagreements about procedures. I won't get into personalities."

"I appreciate that, Natalie."

Ben stood over me now. He sensed the nature of the call.

"Wyatt said to tell you that he sends his best and that he wishes all of you good luck."

"That's very nice of him. And good luck to you and the campaign, Natalie."

"Good-bye, Dev."

"Bye, Natalie."

"She fucking dumped us?"

"Yep," I said, hanging up.

"This late in the campaign?"

"Crane and Wilbur."

"No shit? Well, at least she made a good choice. They're on a roll."

"They're sending an invasion force tomorrow. Six people. They'll want to see everything. According to Natalie, if we help them with the transition, she'll pay all the 'reasonable' bills we submit."

"I love that 'reasonable.' Pure Natalie."

I pushed back from the desk and went to get my coat. Natalie's call hadn't done its damage yet. It probably wouldn't do its worst until the middle of the night when I'd wake up and face the fallout from being fired. I doubted Natalie would keep her word. She'd managed to stick a shiv in us at least once during these interviews. She'd also try to cheapjack us on the bills, denying this one and that one as legitimate expenses. If she said anything especially nasty, we'd have to respond. The public wouldn't care about our battle, but insiders would. Like Susan at her press conference, we'd be on the defensive. We'd have to explain ourselves, and even those who'd been in our position from time to time would pretend otherwise and shake their heads and say poor old Dev must be losing it. It was vanity mostly, I knew. But the image of certain enemies smirking over martinis at the mention of your name was not comforting.

"Where are you going?" Ben said. He sounded plaintive. He didn't want to be alone at this moment, and I didn't blame him. But just because we'd been fired didn't mean I wanted Bobby to sit in jail any longer than he had to.

"I'm sorry, Ben. Sometime tonight steaks and drinks are on me."

"A lot of drinks."

"A lot, a lot."

"Dumped by a fricking starlet," he said. "With one of the greatest asses in history."

I laughed. "So you had fantasies about her, too?"

"You, too? God, how can we hate somebody this much and still want to go to bed with her?"

"A question for the ages, my friend. For the ages."

CHAPTER 21

Rain and darkness hid the grim little strip mall. The only light came from Hair Fare and that was in the back of the shop. I peeked through the window. The front of the place was in shadows. The barber chairs were empty. The light came from the tiny office. I knocked and got no response, so I started pounding.

Sister appeared soon after. She waved and shook her head. With the unlocking of the door came the apology: "I'm so sorry. I didn't hear you. The rain drowns everything out."

"Is Heather still here?"

"Yeah. Sitting in the office. Hurry up. I didn't tell her I asked you to come over. She'll try and get out the back door if she figures it out."

We hurried through the darkness ripe with the scents of hair spray, hair dye, and all the other chemicals used in the various processes.

Sister was right about the bolting. Heather was facing front when I reached the threshold of the office, but when she turned and saw me, she jumped up and said, "No way! Goddamn you, why did you tell him to come here?" Then she lunged at me, palms flat so she could push me away. She was a forceful woman but not forceful enough. I spun her around and dragged her back to her chair and pushed her down in it. Then I slammed the door shut behind us.

"I'm not going to say a single goddamn word to either of you," Heather said, folding her arms across her chest. "We can just sit here all night."

Sister sat behind her desk now. "I did this for your benefit, whether you believe that or not, Heather. You're terrified of something and all you can think of is running away? To where? You don't have any money. I'll bet if I checked your account you'd be overdrawn as usual. And where the hell would you go anyway?"

"To Aunt Sally's." Heather had broken her vow of silence, but now wasn't a good time to point it out.

"Aunt Sally's." Sister found this hilarious. "Between her cooking and his farting, you'd go crazy after one night." Sister looked at me and said, "Aunt Sally gave people food poisoning at three different family reunions over the years. And Uncle Len's always had these gas problems. And it's not just that he farts loud — he smells. We used to have to sit on his lap when we were little, and you just had to hold your breath."

I stood to the left of the desk so that I could see both their faces. Heather couldn't help herself. She smiled at the memory. Sister smiled, too. Her eyes gleamed with tears. "Honey, you got to tell Mr. Conrad here about what you saw. I know you saw something, and I know that you think if you tell anybody, the cops will think you were in on the whole thing."

Heather, blond, blowsy, beaten, now said quietly, "I was in on the whole thing, Sis. I mean, I helped him with things."

"What sort of 'things'?"

Heather's ruined eyes met mine. "I made a couple calls to Cooper's mother. That rich bitch. I disguised my voice though."

"Anything else?" I said.

A long sigh. "I stood in the hallway the night he killed Monica Davies. He wanted me to warn him if anybody came along."

"Oh, God, honey. Oh, God."

Sister's tears reached her cheeks now.

"So he admitted that he killed Monica and took the money?"

"Oh, yeah. He told me all about it. He told me what her face looked like when she was dying."

"What do they call that, Mr. Conrad — assess—"

"Accessory."

"Oh, shit, honey. When Mom finds out —"

We sat in silence. All three of us knew the implications of what she'd just said. Sister started crying now, openly. Put her elbows on her desk and put her face in her hands. She'd been tough and now she was no longer tough, and it was sad to see.

"That's why I want to run away."

You and Bobby, I thought. The pipe dream of Mexico.

Sister snuffled up her tears and sat back in her chair. In the silence, it creaked. "What can she do, Mr. Conrad?"

"The first thing she needs is a lawyer."

"We know one, but he's pretty much a cokehead."

"You mean Larry? The one I dated?"

"Yeah."

"I wouldn't want him as my lawyer. I couldn't even stand him as a boyfriend."

"I guess you weren't listening, Heather. I

wouldn't want him as a lawyer, either. That's why I said he was a cokehead. What's so damned hard to understand about that?" Then: "Sorry I snapped at you. It's just —"

"Let me help you find a lawyer."

Heather's hard gaze met mine. "All this is for Bobby, right?"

"Right."

"And you don't particularly give a shit about what happens to me?"

"I give a shit only to the degree that you tell me everything you know about who killed Donovan in his motel room."

"That's fair," Sister said. "That's damned fair. You help him, he helps you. What the hell's wrong with that?"

Heather traced her fingers across the top of her skull. A sigh exploded from her ripe lips. "I don't know if this means anything or not." She was watching me. "I lied to the cops. I told them I wasn't at Craig's motel last night. But I was. He told me he had some business to take care of and he couldn't see me till morning. Sometimes I'd stop in before work. He never got tired of it, that's one thing you could say for him. You could never wear him out."

"But you went there?"

"Not inside. Not at first. I stood behind a tree — it was like I was back in junior high and following a boy I had a crush on — and just watched. I didn't even care about the rain. I was picturing him in there with a girl. I was really mad. I wasn't there very long before I saw this other guy come out. He was really in a hurry. I wondered why. Dumb me, I thought maybe he was in there on business or something. I didn't think he might've done something to Craig. So when he left I went up to the door. It wasn't closed all the way. I just kind of nudged it with my knee, just enough so I could see inside, you know? And that's when I saw Craig. And I knew he was dead. He was the first dead man I'd ever seen except for people at funerals. But I knew he was dead. And I knew I had to get out of there. I thought maybe the police wouldn't connect me with anything, that maybe I could get by with it. But too many people knew about Craig and me, so the cops found me right away."

"Who was the man you saw?"

She shrugged. "I'm not sure. But I saw the car he was in."

"What kind was it?"

"Some kind of foreign thing, really expensive from the looks of it. It was silver."

There wasn't much doubt about whose car she was describing. But to be sure, I said, "Was it a convertible?"

She sounded curious and surprised. "Yeah. How did you know?"

"Just a lucky guess."

Sister said, "You know who that car belongs to, don't you?"

"Yeah," I said. "Yeah, I do."

Then she looked at Heather. "I hope you're happy, Sis. This is going to tear Mom apart."

But by then I was already at the door and moving fast.

Fog rolled down the streets on my way to foundation headquarters. Streetlights were dulled by ghosts and stoplights burned like evil eyes through the mist. A long stretch of fast-food places shone like a cheap carnival midway in the rolling clouds. And always there was the relentless cold rain, gutters and intersections filling up fast.

Maybe I would have done what Manning did. Maybe I would have started to hate myself so much for being in Natalie's grasp that only an act of violence could make me feel honorable again. Easy to rationalize killing a monster like Craig Donovan. Easy to rationalize taking the money and hiding it until one day you made your escape. People escaped all the time. Just vanished. A good share of them were caught. But some weren't. Some were never heard from again. The lucky ones. The ones who got to start over, clean and whole.

It was funny thinking of the pain he'd feel when he had to give up his sleek new Aston Martin. But he'd have to be careful with his bounty. He could squander it in fast order if he wasn't cautious. There wouldn't be any more Aston Martins in his future unless he was very, very lucky. But he would be free of the stranglehold.

The foundation parking lot held two cars, the Aston Martin and an inexpensive little Ford two-door. I parked near the street end of the lot and reached in for the Glock I'd put in the glove compartment.

The fog on the sidewalk was thick enough to get lost in. Somewhere on the street, headlights tore the fabric of the gray stuff as they headed to the end of the block. Smells of fried chicken from a KFC around the corner. A car radio pounding out rap. Somewhere behind me a pair of cars dueling with their horns. All of it lost in the swamp of gray.

I made my way to the front entrance and tried the door. Unlocked. I went inside and stood on the parquet floor. The only lights on this floor were on the tracks above the framed pieces in the gallery. Keisha's desk was empty.

A churchly quiet was threatened only by my footsteps as I moved through the shadows. The stairs to the second floor looked iconic, like stairs in a movie poster that led the audience to places it shouldn't go. The heating system came on with a tornado of noise.

I eased the Glock from my overcoat pocket and started my way up the wide, curving staircase that ended in what appeared to be impenetrable gloom.

Near the top, trying to make myself alert to even the faintest sound, I heard the first of it. An animal noise. I thought of kittens sick or kittens dying. But it wasn't a kitten, of course. When I reached the top of the stairs and tried to orient myself — I remembered that I turned left to find Manning's office — I heard it again and recognized it for what it was. Another weeping woman.

Between sobs she was talking to somebody. I moved on tiptoe down the hall to the glass-paneled entrance. The reception area was dark. Down the hall behind Doris Kelly's desk I saw a spear of light on the carpet. Manning's office door was open a few inches. I went into the sort of big pantomime movements actors in silent films used. I made it into the reception area and then the hall without being heard. I took a deep breath. I was a silent-movie comic sneaking into a house. I eased the door open just enough to slip through. Then I waited, heart pounding, for any sign that they'd heard me.

I pulled the door closed with great care. I stood there and listened.

"Doris . . . Doris, I followed you last night. The way you were acting . . . so crazy . . . I knew something was wrong." He stopped, sounded as if he was gagging. "You killed him before I could get inside." He was wheezing now as he spoke. There were long rasping pauses between words. "You . . . murdered . . . a . . . man."

But she was angry, unrelenting. "Why do you think I did it? For us. Because I couldn't stand to see you treated the way they treated you. Do you have any fucking idea of the risks I took?"

Quiet little Doris was now furious little Doris. She was shrill. One half octave up and she'd be shrieking.

"I knew about Wyatt taking the money to Monica Davies. I went to her room to get the money, but Donovan beat me to it. Do you have any idea the courage that took? Do you? And then when I killed Donovan and finally got the money — for us — so we could finally go away together — think of what you said to me, David. That I was insane — that this whole thing between us was just my fantasy — that you would have stopped me if you'd known what I was doing — and how the hell do you think that made me feel? After all I went through. After I put my life in jeopardy with scum like Donovan!"

I was on tiptoe again, but I was wondering if either of them would hear me even if I walked on the soles of my shoes. Her voice was about to start shattering glass.

"I did it for us. I thought you'd be happy. I thought we'd finally go away together. I knew you wanted to, even though you wouldn't admit it. I knew it, David. I knew it. I prayed for it and my prayers are always answered. Always, David."

By now I was expecting to hear Manning say something. But there was nothing. Or maybe he couldn't talk. She was speaking in a kind of reverie, the kind I associated with people in alcohol or drug dazes. And maybe she was speaking to a ghost. Maybe Manning was dead.

I took the final four steps to the office door. The space between door and frame was at a bad angle for me. I could see one end of the desk, but I couldn't see Doris or the chairs in front.

"You betrayed me, David. No matter how hard I tried to make you love me, you turned me away. Nobody loved you the way I did, David. Nobody even came close."

I heard him, then. Not words. Just a deep, shaky moan. Then: "Help me, Doris. Help me. Call an ambulance." He sounded as if he'd be sobbing if only he had the strength.

I raised my Glock then raised my foot and gave the door a push so that it opened wide. Then I went in with my gun pointed right at Doris, who sat, prim as always — the wan pretty girl you always wondered about when you sat studying in the library at night, those heartbreaking little legs and that lost nervous gaze — pretty Doris all grown up now.

"Don't move, Doris."

Her eyes remained on Manning, who was slumped in the chair in front of the desk. A bloody hand hung limp, plump drops of blood splashing on the carpet below. As I moved into the office, I kept scanning the desk for any sight of a gun. Her hands were folded and in clear view. I wondered what she'd done with the gun. I could smell the powder in the small confines of the office.

I came around the side of the desk so that

I could see Manning. The pale face and sunken eyes startled me. He had the pallor and pain of one of those beggars you see on TV when those greedy ministers want to soak you for some more tax-free money. I doubted he had much longer to live. From what I could see, he'd been shot in the chest twice. His white shirt was soaked red and something like puke ran down both sides of his mouth. He saw me but he didn't see me. His head gave a little jerk when his eyes and brain came together to recognize me.

He started crying. "Dev — she's crazy, Dev. Never had anything to do with her. Crazy, Dev . . ."

I started to reach for the phone on the desk, but she was faster than me. She grabbed it and hurled it into the air. When it reached the end of its cord length it crashed to the floor. "No! No! I want him dead! All I did for him! All I did for him!"

Kept my Glock on her as I jerked my cell phone from my pocket and punched in 911. I heard myself at one remove talking to the police dispatcher. She was calm and professional. I envied her.

Doris was on her feet, ripping open the middle drawer of the desk. I saw everything in broken images — hand inside the desk — hand coming up — shape and sheen of the .45 — gun being raised.

I went into a crouch and started to pull the trigger of my Glock. All this in mere moments. But then more broken instant images — Doris raising the gun higher, higher — the barrel of the gun gleaming in the overhead lighting — the point of the gun against her head — And then the cry, the plea, the scream. And then the explosion.

Mere moments again as I watched blood and brain and hair freeze for a millisecond in midair, the scream still shocking my entire body. And then in a wild grotesque dance her arms flying out from her body, the gun tossed against the wall, and then the final abrupt death of will and awareness and soul as she collapsed to the floor.

I was shaking and I was cold from sweat freezing on me. I started uselessly toward her, but just then Manning cried out for his mother, and by the time I was able to turn back to him I saw from the terrible angle of his head that he was likely dead.

Sirens, then, coming fast and coming close. There was no point in looking at either of them now. Doris had had her way. She was finally joined with the man she'd never been able to seduce.

CHAPTER 22

SCANDAL TARNISHES A POLITICAL FAM-
ILY.

This story appeared on one of the news
services a week before the election. It was
picked up by hundreds of papers, TV and
radio stations, and, of course, cable news
where talking heads feasted on murder,
blackmail, and the end of what Natalie had
hoped would be a political dynasty. I'm sure
some people said that the story had ensured
Congresswoman Cooper's defeat, but I
think that defeat was inevitable, anyway.
Duffy won by six points; without the story
he might only have won by four or five.

Eight days after the election Natalie
showed up for a half-hour interview with
Larry King. She looked gorgeous. And she
gave great press. She cast herself — as a
writer would — as a concerned but suffering stepmother to an ungrateful stepdaughter whose reckless early years came back to

destroy not only her but poor Natalie as well. All Manning got for his death was a tsk-tsk. She stressed that she'd never liked or trusted Doris and was not surprised that Doris was both a thief and a murderer. She pulled it off with consummate skill. Despite her differences with Susan, she had called her many times over the past months, but Susan would never return her calls. Summoning Tinseltown tears and a scratchy throat, Natalie said, looking directly into the camera, "I still love you, Susan. If you need anything, please call me. Night or day."

In January, Susan vacated her congressional offices and moved to Portland, Oregon, where a college friend of hers ran a public-relations and lobbying firm. There are good lobbies and bad lobbies. This was a good one, its clients working to make life at least marginally better for people society had cast aside.

As for Greg Larson, he found another business partner, and on the day they started smearing people the IRS announced that it was investigating him for tax evasion and tax fraud. He, of course, sputtered about "communists" and this being nothing more than "political revenge," even though the head of the IRS was a Bush appointee who'd stayed on.

And after a while a photo of a tiny pink infant showed up on my Mac screen. Gwen and Bobby, who had also moved to Portland, where Bobby had found work in a supermarket managerial program, had named the boy Devlin Robert Flaherty. "We'll call him 'Dev,' of course," Gwen wrote.

In his first four months in Congress, Duffy surprised many people, including me, by voting for some very liberal bills. We would never have been as savage toward him as the far right proved to be.

I'm writing all this with the scent of pot roast in the air. Jane's here for what she calls her "Chicago weekend," which seems to be a regular thing these days. We swap cooking chores. When it's my turn I take her out to a very expensive restaurant.

I'll be driving back with Jane tomorrow. Sister has asked me to testify on Heather's behalf. She did in fact help find the killer. I'm not sure how much that will help, but I'm willing to do it. The few times I've had to testify in trials I've been nervous and probably not very effective. Maybe I need some pointers. You know, how to give one of those rousing Perry Mason performances where the judge bangs her gavel and proclaims, "This trial is over!"

I imagine Natalie could give me some help with that. But then, she may be too busy. The word is that she'll be announcing Peter's candidacy for Congress very soon now.

I may be wrong, but somehow I don't think she'll be calling me for any help. And even if she did, I wouldn't have the guts to break it to Ben.

ABOUT THE AUTHOR

Ed Gorman is a winner of the Anthony and Shamus Awards. He lives in Iowa.

We hope you have enjoyed this Large Print book. Other Thorndike, Wheeler, Kennebec, and Chivers Press Large Print books are available at your library or directly from the publishers.

For information about current and upcoming titles, please call or write, without obligation, to:

Publisher
Thorndike Press
295 Kennedy Memorial Drive
Waterville, ME 04901
Tel. (800) 223-1244

or visit our Web site at:

http://gale.cengage.com/thorndike

OR

Chivers Large Print
published by AudioGO Ltd
St James House, The Square
Lower Bristol Road
Bath BA2 3SB
England
Tel. +44(0) 800 136919
www.audiogo.co.uk

All our Large Print titles are designed for easy reading, and all our books are made to last.